Future Fiction

Edited by

Francesco Verso

Meteotopia

Futures of Climate (In)justice

A collaboration between CoFutures and Future Fiction

Edited by Bodhisattva Chattopadhyay,

Ana Rüsche and Francesco Verso

Published by Associazione Future Fiction
Via Valentiniano 40 – 00145 Roma
TAX ID: 97962020588

Special thanks go to Sandro Mattioli, professor at the International School of Comics in Rome, who collaborated with Future Fiction in the creation of the contest for the cover and internal illustrations that enrich this anthology.

This work is part of the project "CoFutures: Pathways to Possible Presents". The project is funded by the European Union's Horizon 2020 research and innovation program under grant agreement no. 852190 (ERC Starting Grant 2019).

Title: *Meteotopia – Futures of Climate (In)justice*
© 2022 Future Fiction, Roma
ISBN: 9788832077483
I edition July 2022
info@futurefiction.org

Illustration by Nicole Maione

Environmentalism often maintains the dispossession of Indigenous peoples for the common good of the world.

Jodi Byrd

Our world is full of largely irremediable unfairnesses. The scale of the pressures on communities around the world is quickly ratcheting up, and in many cases is already far beyond the capacities of even wealthy countries to lever down, meaning more and more of the world is becoming brittle in the face of the planetary crisis.

Alex Steffen

Meteotopia serves as a focus for several concerns we have in the project CoFUTURES: Global South futurisms, environmental futures, climate justice, and thinking from the margins. The spaces of fiction and fictionality also allow us to play with the concerns of our presents but not merely from an academic perspective, but from an inspirational and aspirational perspective to imagine better futures. Putting together this anthology thus has been a labour of love: eight different works of fiction are on offer, with writers from Botswana, Brazil, Nigeria, Senegal, Mexico, Phillippines, and India. Some writers are established names, others lesser known to the non-Anglophone world. There are also works in translation here.

The anthology itself is funded by and part of the project led by me, "CoFutures: Pathways to Possible Presents," which is financed by the European Research Council. CoFutures is the first project ever on global science fiction to be funded by the European Research Council, and without a doubt the single largest research project on this theme around the world. Its success is a testament not only to the changing landscape of research on speculative future fiction, but also to emergence of the field of Co-Futurisms. This financing has allowed us, for this volume, to gather stories, art, make translations, and finally offer the book as a completely open access volume. I will also add that this is our first anthology project, with many more to come in the next years. To learn more about us, go to https://cofutures.org.

Partnering with Future Fiction to bring out the anthology was a natural choice, given their commitment to producing and highlighting the contemporary range of speculative writing globally. I am grateful to all the authors, artists, and translators, and especially thankful to Francesco Verso and Ana Rüsche as co-editors for joining me on this adventure, and to Vita Kvedaraite for all her administrative help that made this book possible. A special thanks to the Department of Culture Studies and Oriental Languages, University of Oslo, for being the host for the CoFutures project.

I hope you enjoy the book as much as we did putting it together. We would love to hear from you what you think, so please reach out to us at the project.

Live long and prosper
Bodhisattva Chattopadhyay

Introduction

by Francesco Verso and Ana Rüsche

The relationship between man and nature is a very ancient one and has always had two main characteristics since the dawn of time: respect and domination.

That unknown natural force, whose delicate and complex mechanisms man has gradually revealed and understood, has always remained an essential element in planning and programming of any aspect of human life: agriculture, navigation, engineering, to name just a few, are disciplines that couldn't be separated from the knowledge of nature and its real functioning. And often it was necessary to make a huge effort of the imagination, a leap into the darkness of the most incredible fantasy, to be able to discover what was hidden behind the veil of natural appearances.

The geological eras have followed one another without humankind's existence, with humanity having no say in the formation of the planet. Then, from our appearance, it took us thousands of years before we became aware of our position within the great fresco of nature. This perception of finitude, which has often been accompanied by an almost sacred sense of respect for the environment, lasted for millennia and it is only in the last few centuries that an anthropocentric vision of the world has imposed itself in all advanced Western societies, causing a radical change in the relationship between man and nature.

Domination overwhelmed respect. Exploitation overwhelmed management. And so science stripped nature of its ancient mysteries, rendering it naked and defenseless against anyone who wanted to appropriate its resources. The industrial revolution established itself as a model of predatory ecological abuse and, from then on, everything changed. Efficiency, productivity and limitless growth have become the "mantras of modernity", in defiance of any other concept of justice and the principle of long-term sustainability. However, it is precisely science – over the last century – that has finally realized its immense power and its responsibility towards nature and has attempted – often remaining *vox clamantis in deserto* – to remedy its ability to modify without compensation, and thus contributing to the formation of a widespread scientific awareness, a sort of mass environmental consciousness which, perhaps, will be able to curb the human greed that has been unleashed by the great ideologies of the twentieth century, communism and capitalism: the first imploded on the presumption of building a society free from earthly needs with which to transcend materialism, the second proposed itself as a short-term material solution capable of solving anything through the market. Both, however, have underestimated, if not overlooked and often abused, natural resources.

It is precisely today, when the concept of capitalism seems to have no enemies, that it is time to re-imagine the future of the relationship between man and nature. Precisely today that human behaviors, for good and especially for bad, have such profound consequences for the ecosystem in which we all live – so much so that we have entered what many call the geological era of the Anthropocene (and Plantationocene and Capitalocene) – it is essential to rethink what is right and what is not right to do, and also to ask oneself how far it is legitimate to go and, above all, by what means?

In the essay "Capitalist Realism" Mark Fisher perfectly illustrates the idea: "Wall-E presents a version of this fantasy – the idea that the infinite expansion of capital is possible, that capital can proliferate without labor – on the off world ship, Axiom, all labor is performed by robots; that the burning up of Earth's resources is only a temporary glitch, and that, after a suitable period of recovery, capital can terra form the planet and recolonize it."

Is imagining something different today really that impossible? Is even just hypothesizing a non-capitalist system really a sterile, useless exercise, devoid of real foundations, almost the ambition of a nostalgic hippie? In fact in recent years mainstream contemporary literature, with rare exceptions – in its psychoanalytic drift and in a progressive sliding towards a disenchanted postmodernism – has forgotten that, quoting Fisher again: "environmental disaster features in late capitalist culture only as a kind of simulacra, its real implications for capitalism too traumatic to be assimilated into the system. The significance of Green critiques is that they suggest that, far from being the only viable political-economic system, capitalism is in fact primed to destroy the entire human environment. The relationship between capitalism and eco-disaster is neither coincidental nor accidental: capital's 'need of a constantly expanding market,' its 'growth fetish', means that capitalism is by its very nature opposed to any notion of sustainability."

So where to look for other possible worlds and viable solutions? Science fiction has the ambition to describe what doesn't yet exist, but which – under certain conditions – could happen. Science fiction writers place themselves as excellent builders of future worlds with dark and elusive features but also with hopeful and strategic solutions. Science fiction inhabits domains of tomorrow and thanks to this looking-forward vocation it knows its strengths and weaknesses. That's why we asked eight Science Fiction writers from seven countries of the Global South to give us their visions of *climate (in)justice*: because Science Fiction stories have the unique ability to imagine something different from reality, and to challenge the concreteness of the present.

Illustration by Valentina Paliotta

Eco-humans

by Tlotlo Tsamaase

Tlotlo Tsamaase is a Motswana writer (xe/xem/xer or she/her pronouns). Tlotlo's novella, *The Silence of the Wilting Skin*, is a 2021 Lambda Literary Award finalist and was shortlisted for a 2021 Nommo Award. Xer story "Behind Our Irises" is the joint winner of the Nommo Award for Best Short Story (2021), the first Motswana to win the award. Xer short story "Dreamports" was longlisted for a BSFA Award. Xer short fiction has appeared in *The Best of World SF Volume 1, Clarkesworld, Terraform, Africanfuturism Anthology, The Year's Best African Speculative Fiction (2021), Apex Magazine* and is forthcoming in *Africa Risen* and *Chiral Mad 5*, Rich Horton's *The Year's Best Science Fiction and Fantasy, 2021 Edition* and other publications. Xe was the first Motswana to be a 2017 Rhysling Award nominee. Xe is a 2011 Bessie Head Short Story Award winner. You can find xem at tlotlotsamaase.com and on Instagram and Twitter at @tlotlotsamaase.

Air prices have risen. *Again.*

650 degrees, the sun wavers in that summer blue. A few years young *ago* it was big, warm, a bright spot dribbling arcs across the winter blue.

Now. Six hours left I have of my body. My skin wrinkles; baked earth cracked from the summer drought. The pixel panels line my skin like rash. They peel at the edges. The sunlight falls heavily through the pores. But blood and sunlight are oil and water, mix they do not.

"Close the curtains," lover boy moans. The bed squeaks as he turns under our love-making sheets.

"Close. The curtains," I repeat, a staccato whisper. A hummingbird is caged in my ribs. Fast, fast, fast it flaps rushing for a never-coming explosion. Time leaks open a fear-wound I'm afraid to heal: I have to go.

Loverboy, underneath the brown, lovemaking sheets, snores. His body is jaunty. Beneath his skin his bones are wiry. They hurt me.

[close the curtains]

But the sunrise is warm, an inviting fire in the skyline. And soon Botswana's notorious heat will climb our backs, will suffocate us into a terrifying dizzying until we don't know what oxygen is. I stare at my lover. The last time I picked words from his lips *[I love you]* I failed to put them back. To forget them from my own body would be to peel my skin and wrap it around his eyes *[to blind them from my secrets that poison my beauty daily]* and leave me naked for the sun to burn.

Dung, shit, mud: the walls encircle us like we're covered beneath the earth; thatch seals this coffin of ours shut. Cow shit—little hardened poops of cow—I picked, sparse-spread in the Malokogonyane village, and handed to *Nkuku* and watched her make this heart—hut—of ours. The memory hardens the pain in my chest, for I miss her, miss the life she could've had if only she'd survived long enough to get her air supply.

My hands scale over the knobs of my backbone to refill the finishing sanctioned air contained in my lungs. "5 hours and 55 minutes of air remaining," says the operator in my mind, her voice carrying a Zimbabwean accent, "please pay you air bill to receive an oxygen refill." My hands are wet, my throat is tight. Breathing makes me cough; it forms traffic with the words in my throat. This is probably how *Nkuku* felt before she left us. I remember how weightless and feeble her body felt when we carried her from the fields where she'd collapsed. Her skin so wrinkled and paper-soft. Her veins, thick and visible, no longer throbbing with life. I don't want to go like her, with so much of my life undiscovered. But if I die now, would I meet her in the afterlife? Maybe the afterlife is heaven compared to this life we're living.

"I...can't," I want to say, "do this anymore."

My vision blurs, the tears sting like onion tears. My fingers stumble on the knobs of my spine.

Please work. Please, *tswee.*

White noise inflames my brain, ears, and eyes. The filter in my throat has cracked. Air wheezes through, quickly and faintly, touching at the lining of my tube to my lungs. I must get it fixed. With what money? My breaths sprout from my cracked, peeling lips. The day they decided to recognize us as sentient as humans, as citizens of this planet was the day we had to fend for ourselves. If you didn't come from a wealthy family—families that stretched their lifespans over centuries by fusing their biology with ours—you were on your own. We were half-them, half-us with subpar skills that could hardly obtain us creative jobs. Too defective for factory jobs or similar work. Whereas a human could starve themselves for a few days and still live, or go without water for short periods, we couldn't starve ourselves of sunlight, oxygen or nutrients for longer than a day. We'd die, and they'd recycle us for the next possessor. Maintaining my life, this body, is higher than the rent I pay for my tiny abode. The only job I could get was at Better Us Tech, allowing experiments on the tampering of my biology, with little remuneration. It's the only way I can fuel my body, to keep it running. They need it running to better assess their experiments to develop a better us and a more efficient eco-human than our failed versions. One day they won't need me. Until then I need to find a solution.

"Babe, don't worry. The shelter could always give you another body," lover boy says. "Sleep like me."

The shelter is the only right we have, the right to live, to continue to suffer in this world. But the bodies we receive from the shelter are low-caste and defective. Diseases are rife in those systems that you're as good as a zombie. For health security purposes, such bodies' movements are restricted to particular districts where there's no running water, the sewage stinks the place out, and the infrastructure appears like dizzy torsos in the sky always leaning to and fro, like they're gossiping with each other. Those districts are the hub of factory workers, where labor is extracted for textiles, clothing and beauty products for this beloved city.

As if he can read my mind, lover boy leans on his elbow. "The shelter isn't a bad place. At least you'll still get to live."

"I don't want the wrong freedom. The wrong body," I fail to say.

Crumpled paper makes it into my hands. My nails scratch words. Red-blood words bleed from my fingers to form a

Grocery list:
#1 Air.
#2 Sunlight.
#3 Joy.
#4 Love.
Quotas of the month run out from my body. 365 days I want of the warm, golden sunlight. The kind that does not burn the blood. Yet air, sunlight, joy and love stand around us freely, but to receive the utilities of this body I must pay for a
doctor's appointment:
#1 Hate,
#2 anger,
#3 jealousy
#4 etc.
Renewable utilities. Renewable germs.

The skin-pixel panels are growing old, too old to absorb any more of the sunlight. The stress forces an itch to my skin. The solar heat is too strong for it. The veins underneath curl away, *thicken:* a migraine needles through my brain.

The automated network voice-over synced to my credit levels blares from my speaker ears so that lover boy complains about the noise. "Warning. This is an infraction code. You do not have enough credit to live. Your rental pay for the body is used up. Visit your nearest clinic to correct the transaction. Failure to follow instructions will have your blood supply blocked *warra-warra* blah blah" it goes.

Warning! I sing-song. *Warra-warra.* This is my family's last living property. My body; my last heirloom. I cannot *lose* it. I have to go.

Three hours left I have of my body. The sun has knocked off. A piece of its hibiscus ribbons lies behind, cutting tales into the dainty sky. Loverboy sleeps. He never has to worry about losing his body. His family's estate keeps their children with a constant supply of bodies, from people willing to sell their own, backdoor sales. But only a certain type: healthy, good looking and young. Yes, money can't buy love but it can keep you immortal. Is that why I'm with him? Stupid enough to believe in our love? That I will be his Mrs. one day? And he'll be in a desperate need for me that I'll be in supply of those bodies they have access to. Wealth and youth, within my grasp. I close my eyes, shut the fantasies into a dark place inside me. He'll never love me. I'm just a body. To use and enjoy. Unless I use the trick that other girls perform to trap men like him. I can't believe I've fallen this far to resort to that. *I disgust myself.* Anyway, the trick doesn't work. The family allows you to carry the baby then take it away as soon as you give birth. You're only a surrogate for their heir even if that heir carries your genes. Us low-caste people are only good enough to sleep with, not introduce into their family. He wakes three hours later. I have three hours to make

love

to my lover boy, sweet love. His house in Good Hope is walls of brick; pale, pink shingles the hue of a soft, pink-tinged sunlight shelter his home. Dated wood frames the windows. The house rises, rises, rises until I can't stare any further up without the sun melting into my eyesight. And I wonder how it feels to be so wrapped in wealth, to douse yourself in so much luxury than you need that you become so bored you resort to entertaining yourself with a person like me. With things that trip your mind. With things that could kill you. To cling to such wealth with absurd addiction as if everyone's out to get you. His wealth lazes around his vineyards, the agricultural fields, and his bank accounts with nothing to do except to watch the poor streets from the balcony of his pride. Sometimes he keeps his safe open to lewdly drink my expression of hunger as I ogle his wads of cash and gold. I know that he only wants me around to remind himself how above me he is, that I can be the rock-bottom he tussles with in bed, so he can tell his friend on a scale of 1–10 how I rate against the women from his class.

The breeze tickles my ankles, startling me from my thoughts. Inside his yard, a three-legged dog—teeth sharpened by sweet-love's knives—barks and barks, saliva spilling out from between its teeth and gums. I once watched sweet-love snip off its tail with pruning shears. Claws against the fence, a dirty yellow, shake the fence: music of claw against metal rings. Dog and I aren't on good terms for we starve for its master's love. This is our consistent conversation:

Dog: If it weren't for this fence…you would be dead.

Me: I'll have him cut your heart out and bake it into a pie.

Dog glares. I glare.

The mahogany door pulls open. Two hours left leave me with a panic, but his image stops the flow of my blood; my *mokwerekwere.* His breath stains my lips, the canvas of our illicit… He's showered in rain and baked earth. His skin, smooth of pixel panels, give off a glimmer like a moon rises from within his body. I want to touch him. He stills me. He makes me warm, unlike lover boy sleeping in our half-empty bed. I turn to dog and hope it reads the look in my eyes: You can't love him back. I can.

A hot, burning hunger grumbles in my stomach when I see white porridge, a ring of bright, yellow margarine melting in the middle, sitting on a wooden desk. A *koboko* or *sjambok* with chains and cuff hangs on a rustic brick wall in the lounge suspiciously, an intimate décor for a BDSM playroom. My shoulders shrink up and down at the thought of being in that room. What is free—locked in this skin, locked under this blue, locked by gravity on this ground we crawl? Wings cripple the white of this bone. My *mokwerekwere* boy, I don't know his name but I call him *Moks.*

Moks wastes no time, he carves his way into me that, watching our shadows lovemaking on the wall—a moonlight shadow art—the candle moves about tickled and caressed by the heated sounds, inflating the burdened air that presses up against the windows; a fog from within a box. The souls, the shadows are effervescent to the touch of fire. They fight against the walls. The dark and night are two different humans. But love enters, taciturn. And maybe in some far universe, this is how people fuel their lives. *This* is where I'd rather die, rather than on a dust-laden street with shells of poverty flanking its pathways.

The edges of the night are frail and contain little of us. My body weakens from the derailing blood supply but worse from the guilt. Loverboy, unaware of this as my fortnightly occupancy, still lies asleep in our half-empty bed.

Sleep comes with a dreadful foreign trade-off. I'm too poor to dream. I force my eyes open to the remaining time I have, 13 minutes, blinking in red lights against my eyeballs. They—warning, warning *warra-warra*—steal from us, use sleep as a natural defector. Renting into their dream state comes steeply. My passport is filled with divided lands of memories, wishes, family and lucid dreaming like picking a channel from a subscription TV service. I cannot visit; I don't want to fall asleep.

The walls segregate the dreamless and the dreaming. The point of segregation does not lie far away. My eye rolls back at its own volition, pop-ups driving it crazy. That's my fault for buying trial visual programs to decode the scenery. At this point, everything comes at a blur: a hallucination of moving trees naked of leaves. I wake. Sit up. Watch him sleep. The flickering of his eyes beneath the curtain of his eyelids. I trace my fingers across his face as if my hand will be able to taste his dreams. I watch the vein in his neck tick, tick, tick, the wealth of his blood streaming through it. Instantly, I'm overwhelmed with anger and incredible hate. *He* could save. *He* could save me. Does he want me to get on my knees and beg?

I take a deep breath and nudge him. "Love, they will take my body."

I push *Moks* awake. He groans, stretches and yawns. He eyes the unfinished gold liquor in his shot glass, swallows it in one gulp and his breath is hot with intoxication.

"*My* body you mean." He smiles. His fingers pinch my breast. "*This* is mine."

Shame doesn't shut my mouth; hunger for survival pulls my lips open, "I need rent money to keep it. To stay. I have seven minutes left."

"Come back to bed. Leave the night alone." His skin is papery thin. Translucent. His fingers tug at my skin. "Stop *jolling* with that boy and stay with me. *Leave* him. Keep me."

His words are crude; his words are salt harshly seasoning my fortnights. Pink veins streak across his forearms. The sun lives in his chest, beating but thrashing at times—*that* human part I want.

My thoughts tear me to an *ago* time:

Humans once stood under the night sky, skinny as birches, palms reaching out to the falling moonlight. Moonshine strings fell freely into their hands and into their pores enriching their old-age blood. Some barely acknowledged it. I'd barter a lung, a heart and five fingers for that celestial milk that would give smoothness to my broken skin.

I had a dream once that moonshine tasted like marshmallows—a soft pillow of sweetness encasing scented air; and if I stretched high enough, stood on my tip-toes until my calves ached, I'd touch the sky and run free like a shooting star in rewind back to where it came from.

But eco-humans are limited to consuming a cupful of moonlight; the heart is starved and stout, quantities of love are non-essential until it's all we have left.

I want to lie in this bed with *Moks* forever, in this richness devoid of poverty, staring at the ceiling fan whirring, eyes burning from trying to count the revolutions each blade makes. Cold tears creep out from my eyes. I'm too tired to breathe to live, because to live is to struggle.

Moonlight and sunlight are kicks of protein and carbohydrates my body craves. My great-great-great-grandmother had the gift of air, water and sky abundant to her before the world changed and took it from her body. Nightmares of man's evolution into destruction haunt my cellar brain: a hole has been raped into the ozone layer; humans are compacted into a biofuel battery, a power source of the blue summer ceiling to patch the hole in my heart.

"I can't leave him," my voice cries. "Please, I only have three minutes left."

Moks leans on his elbow. His lashes are long and his eyes are a rare blue gem.

His words are crude: "Choose to live or die. I am life and that boy is death. What man can't protect his woman. Choose me *woman!*"

His breath is pure; his love my opiate.

Riding on another's back is a habit *Nkuku* boxed my ears for. My ears sting as though she stands in this room in a flesh, wrinkles sagging her brownness.

If I choose him, I enter a forever prison. He'll own even my afterlife. So, I decline and I press my hands flat on the crinkled sheets and recite *Nkuku*'s words: "Every man is allowed to dig his own grave, walk faithfully to it, pull the blanket of earth to his neck and sleep." I face *Moks*, my nakedness a sacrilege to his pure one, realizing the decision I make is prison too. "I want to sleep."

\#

Sunlight is heavy when it meets the cloth over my bones. I don't fret that lover boy will wonder on my disappearance. That my weak lies would still lure forgiveness from him like sourcing kindness from evil. The sunlight is heavy; my body heats up, my blood lights up red, green, and amber. My bones will break from the inside, their shards will kill me.

"Warning. This is an infraction code. You do not have enough credit to live. Your blood supply has been blocked, your reservoir oxygen will last fifty seconds *warra-warra* blah blah" it goes.

I stare at *Moks*, his lips slightly parted, blowing pillows of cool air into my face. The pins and bones that hold his skin together mock mine for their brittleness and tectonics. The horizon where each skin pixel meets the next is seamless, like the color blue that invades our ceiling. The world remains silent waiting for the hour of sun to return back to work.

"Tell me," I devote my last words to a sleeping *Moks*, "what do they pay that sparkling globe in the sky? Human as us, it nourishes itself. Cannibals, we ate the earth now, the mortar that ties that ceiling together cracks. Look." I open the curtain wider. "The blue ceiling warps like a shooting star trying to prick its way to us. One day, *Moks*, I want that invisible shield, that glass to shatter, stab us with its shards."

He stirs from bed, yawns and stretches. Again. Must have been an expensive dream. Deftly, like eating with knife and fork, he cuts words into my ears. The receiver responds slowly, the message takes long to reach my brain. Impatient, he leaves the bed, butt-naked and muscular. My nails claw the air but fail to reach his last scent, the ghostly fabric that warps from his skin. One day I'll have the scent-fabric to hold, taste, wear and sew it to the edge where my skin ends.

That pain that wakes me at night, that frightens my lover boy, pricks me by day, deforms my bones by evening. *Moks* drips water from his shower. The white ash-bone peeks out beneath the seams of his skin tightly sewn to his clogged breath. He coughs it out onto his hands and feeds me carefully like a thirsty baby. He does love me.

The smoke-breath spouts back into his gauzed lips. The smoke seeking its refuge—the lung, the hung—ghostly strings hatched into the skull forming tresses of fire down his face, his neck, his jaw—the sun falls down, failing to pull back its fires.

Moks is hungry. Again. His teeth—little claws of the soul—seek an opening into my skin, seeks the other-half-soul torn like a ghostly garment lost in the Botswana heat. My skin lets loose a sunset liquid down the knobs of limbs in-between our secrets.

Choose life or death.

My head shakes: "An honest man digs his own grave and walks to it faithfully."

The suns scales through the blue sky. I am perfect, irregular at the joints. The first time a boy touched me my skin inflamed. Now the pixel panels peel out from the edges like a scab. Don't scratch. Don't scratch.

Moks's breath clogs into my ear. I can feel the wet of his saliva sticking into the inner walls of my ears. "Choose: him or me. Life or death. Heirloom or love." I stare at his brick walls. "Decide tonight before you leave or don't bother coming back."

I ponder on my maternal family:

We have a curse in our family. We call the aunts the first generation and the cousin the second and us—the children of the first—the third. Love is a hard-to-come-by renewable energy. The aunts are divorced, lost their husbands, or their husbands ran free. My lover boy, a potential husband, lies in our heart made by the wrinkled hands of *Nkuku.*

He waits for me.

He loves me.

"Who will pay for your body huh," *Moks* asks. "I will take care of you. Choose. I refuse to share… anymore." His hands touch my naked stomach as I wrap my arms around my breasts.

The curse makes my family but do I abide to this curse to make me?

Do I choose: *Moks*, life, and heirloom or lover boy, death, and love? My body must not get repossessed.

[An honest man digs his grave.]

"I… can't," I want to say, "do this anymore." My pulse throbs from a voltage fluctuation.

Illustration by Edoardo Mozzin

Island of Jaguars

by Toni Moraes

translated by G. Holleran

Toni Moraes is a Latin American man born in 1986 in Belém do Pará, Amazon region, northern Brazil. He graduated in Architecture and Urbanism at the Federal University of Pará and has worked in the publishing market since 2015. He is editor of Monomito Editorial, publishing contemporary literature from Brazil and other Latin American countries, with special attention to the various aspects of fantastic literature. In 2017 he published the novel "*O ano em que conheci meus pais*" (The year I met my parents) and in 2018 the book of short stories "*Eu estou morto*" (I am dead). In addition to these publications, he has participated in several collections of short stories in Brazil and Spain. He is a master's student in the Brazilian Literature program at the Faculty of Philosophy, Letters and Human Sciences at the University of São Paulo, where he studies aspects of violence in the work "Cinzas do Norte", by the writer Milton Hatoum.

Honey flowed from the gourd in a perennial strand and, permeated by the scarce light that cast a glow on the funeral grounds, tinged everything it touched with amber. Kneeling on the floorboards, Anahy directed the viscous-sweet voluptuousness like Iara, the Mother of the Waters, handling a river's momentum—anointing the deceased cacica from whom she would inherit leadership over the jaguar-women. Around her, the other warrior women were chanting their song of passage, waiting for the moment to cut off locks of their hair, dark as the heart of the forest, with which to adorn their leader's body that lay on the mat. This would allow her to cross unharmed to the other plane before the eyes of the Mother Jaguar, who since the beginning of time has, in her avarice, devoured everything she does not recognise as kin.

"My netas—my granddaughters—one day this will be you, from pouring the honey to lying in repose on the mat. It is the destiny of all of the jaguar-women, of all the Kunhãyawaretê. When your day arrives, this ritual is the respect you will pay to each other and to all our people. With it, we honour the bravery of each jaguar-warrior who helped to build everything that makes us today, each one of our grandmothers, our avós who fought for this land that gives us everything, since the very first of them, who came from the Mother Jaguar's womb and planted the first manioc tree in these parts, lit the first fire, and established the first settlement. That is why it is so important for you to be here, truly be here, so you can commune with the spirits who bring us wisdom."

Standing with the other warriors, Bartyra knew that her elder's words were meant for her specifically, even though she was not the only one witnessing a rite of passage for the first time, an honour reserved only for those women who were already initiated into the ancient combat knowledge of the jaguar warriors. The girl's attention was split between the delicacy that dripped from the gourd, a rarity after bees had disappeared from most parts of the world, and the screen on her wristband, which she was using to track a motorboat racing across the broad river towards the island. The lenses of the vulture-like urubudrones that keep watch over the Guajará Bay from the opposite bank of the river, on the coast of the megalopolis Belém, had flagged the boat for going more quickly than advisable for that crossing.

The young warrior recognized the vessel; its engine was one she had developed, produced with the island's technology and powered by biofuel, but this did not reassure her. She had been taught from an early age to always be alert, to be suspicious of everything, especially if it came from the other side of the river.

"Bartyra!" scolded Anahy, snapping the youth out of her swirling thoughts and speculations.

"I'm sorry, my avó. It's just that there's someone headed here, I think it's the…"

"Whatever it is, it can wait." The elder stood up and walked over to the girl, holding a small ceramic pot in one hand and a spine from a pupunheira palm tree in the other. "Here." She handed the objects to the young warrior with a firm gaze and the deliberate motions of someone not constrained by the construct of time. "Since Mayara was part of your clan, you will be doing the painting."

Bartyra was surprised, but she knew what to do. Any of the other women there would have known, too. Only the deceased elder warrior's face would remain uncovered by locks of hair pasted to the honey that coated her body. It was up to the new cacica to choose the bravest member of the deceased's clan to carry out the mortuary face painting, the finishing touch in adorning the jaguar-woman for her rite of passage.

Such a gesture implied great responsibility. Being chosen to do the painting also meant assuming the role of the deceased's madrinha, who conducts the rest of the funeral rites, from burial in a ceramic urn to composting the body's remains, which would be spread over the soil in the Forest of Spirits to enrich and fertilise it.

"Do you still remember which ybyrá tree Mayara chose?" Anahy asked, knowing that no jaguar-women in their leader's clan would forget such important information, the same way you don't forget the name of someone you live with. It also falls to the madrinha of the deceased to plant the seedling that will shelter the jaguar-warrior's soul on earth in the Forest of Spirits, and to watch over its development for life.

"I do, my avó, it was the Samaumeira," Bartyra responded, and her mind wandered to the Mayara-ybyrá, whose colossal roots, many years from now, would rise from the earth to create a refuge for the coming generations of jaguar-women to meditate in search for the wisdom of their ancestors.

Bartyra resisted the urge to check the screen on her wristband one last time and took her place by the side of the deceased. Using jenipapo fruit extract, she began to paint that face that even after life retained the dignity and serenity of the leader the woman had been. Each of the two clans had its own distinct artwork, but both had the same purpose: to transfer to the face of the fallen warrior the features and qualities of a yawaretê, a jaguar.

As she honed in on her task, which she performed under the crowd's mournful silence, Bartyra was overcome with echoes of the words that had surrounded her since she was a little girl. What the elders told of the history of their people, and the history of the world itself, was no small matter.

One of these teachings in particular had always sent her mind spinning. She used to like hearing when one of her mothers or grandmothers, running her hands through her hair, much more interested in stroking it than in picking out lice and nits, sang the tragedy of Pu'puña, who earned the disfavour of the Mother Jaguar by transforming herself, after death, into a tree that bore delicious fruit, but had a trunk full of thorns. When she tried to enjoy the fruit, the Mother Jaguar's whole body was mangled, and her skin never healed from the marks of her defeat. As she licked her wounds, she cursed all of Pu'puña's daughters, who from that moment forward would never be able to transform into jaguars to hunt or defend themselves. That, said the elders, was the reason why the kunhãyawaretê jaguar-women had lost their ability to shapeshift and had to resort to this funerary ritual.

Her mind still filled with memories, the girl finished painting and stood up. Then the other kunhãs, except for Anahy, started to cut strands of their hair and stick them to the body of the deceased, separating the strands so as not to lose or waste any material. Bartyra looked around for the elder, but she was nowhere to be found.

Outside of the stilt house, which stood a metre and a half above the waterlogged ground, like all the buildings in that part of the island, which had been dry land before the water rose, Anahy passed her fingers over the ecopanels on the wall, protected from the drizzle by the eaves that shielded the whole structure. She noticed the girl approaching.

"One day I'll go to the laboratory just to see how you turn that pile of açaí pits into these beauties." Anahy noted the detailed way the pieces fit together.

"My plans for açaí fibre are even bigger than that, my avó. You'll see… before long, we'll be able to do incredible things with it."

"I'm sure we will, my neta." Anahy turned toward the girl, a hint of a smile in the subtle curves of her lips. She came closer and stared at her in silence, her eyes scrutinising. "Bartyra, do you know why I chose you?"

"I think I do, avó." Bartyra was well aware of Anahy's fear, of the distrust that the five years she spent away from the community had caused in the elder.

"You haven't been the same since you've returned, my neta. You spend all day holed up at the college, in front of a screen, talking to the outsiders who hosted you, and you forget to live with our sisters, you forget our rituals, you forget that life isn't just measured by charts, numbers, essays. I'm not saying that what you do is meaningless, far from it. Everybody knows that your research is important—not just for the folks who live here on the Island of Jaguars, but for everyone, kin or not, who cares about what happens to this land." Anahy was firm in her gaze and in her words. "But if you're not connecting with the folks in our village, how are you going to understand the concerns of those who live here, of our people? Who will your research be for if you're not one with what surrounds you? Everything that we and our grandmothers built and struggled to maintain, the community college, the laboratories and biotech workshops, our relationships with the outside institutions that received you, all of this was done for one reason alone...."

"To guarantee the survival of our people..." Bartyra interjected.

"Not only that, my grandchild, but to ensure that we can live on our ancestral land, with our customs, with our culture, without depending on the greed of those who confuse prosperity with death and destruction."

Despite their age difference and belonging to different clans that separated them in even the most routine village tasks, Anahy and Bartyra shared a great closeness. The elder commanded the defence force of the jaguar warriors. It was she who trained the young ones of the village in the art of Kunhãyawaretê combat, she who taught them to be as much a part of the forest as the foliage surrounding them and to defend their territory with the same agility and precision that the jaguar uses to defend her young. And if there was one thing that hadn't changed about Bartyra, it was how interested and dedicated she was to everything Anahy taught, and she once again listened to her elder attentively.

"The Mother Jaguar is cheeky, my neta, and her plans are a mystery to us, but when the creature wants something, all we can do is willingly submit. I sense that one day it will fall to you to lead our people, because the Mother Jaguar prefers valiant warriors. But when it's your turn, Bartyra, there can be no doubt in your heart, and I know your chest is heavy with fear. This isn't the first time I've encountered a jaguar-warrior like you."

Bartyra's eyes welled up. Anahy widened her smile that before had just been an outline, a grin that, more than anything, was welcoming and affectionate. The girl hugged her and her tears dampened the elder's shoulders.

"I don't know what's happening, avó, I don't… I don't feel like I…" Bartyra struggled between sobs.

"Belong here?" Anahy finished.

The girl couldn't bring herself to answer. For that moment, all the two embracing jaguar-warriors could hear was the drumming of the accumulating rain, accompanying the melody of the women who continued to honour the dead cacica in the rite of passage. Then Anahy pulled away from Bartyra, who was wiping her eyes, and continued:

"My neta, all that those men on the other side want, have always wanted, is to make us believe that we have to stop being who we are and become what they think we should be. They think we belong in a space that is not our culture, but will never fully be theirs, either. They want to hijack our identities, everything that makes us. Look around you… Look, my neta." Bartyra peered over her shoulder and back at the elder. "You are everything around you, and everything around you is you, too. Our people only exist because we resist as one, our people, our customs… Those from the outside will always try to break our link with our culture, with our land, with our kin… They will try to take away our right to be as we are. But as long as one of us lives, we all live. As long as this land keeps giving us manioc for our flour and good ybyrá wood for our arrows, we resist. So don't worry, Bartyra, there is time yet for your heart to find serenity. This is the only way you will truly feel what you have never at any moment ceased to be: a kunhãyawaretê warrior."

Anahy kept gazing warmly at Bartyra as she dried her tears.

"Thank you, my avó."

She took the elder's hands in hers and kissed each one before feeling a light vibration from her wristband. It was a message from the guard at the pier: "Kayky's worried sick looking for you. I told him to wait at the college. Better take Anahy too. Sounds like it's serious."

Anahy hesitated, not wanting to step away from the ritual, but the grave tone of the message convinced her. As they stepped in silence along the wooden walkways that led to the college, the rain cooled down, hanging in the air, aggravating the warmth they felt in their bodies. Even though they were supposedly in the Amazonian winter, which once had soaked each breath with its humidity and lowered the temperature by a few degrees, this was the first rain they'd had in days.

When they got to the college, Kayky, the pilot of the speedboat that Bartyra had recognised, was waiting for them outside. Wearing the customary midnight blue, his hand alternated between scratching his head and reaching into his trouser pocket. He couldn't wait any longer for them to come closer and hurried to meet them.

"I ask for the spirits' blessing and protection, my avó," Kayky said as he kissed Anahy's right hand.

"May they bless and protect you, my neto."

"I saw your motorboat coming in at full speed, Kayky. What happened? Why the rush? You couldn't have sent a message first?" Bartyra could no longer hide her anxiety.

"I'm coming from the State Court of Justice, Baty—the judge gave an injunction for Velásquez & Andrade to take control of the island! I had to come here personally to warn you, so I did, as fast as I could."

Bartyra raised her hands to her forehead. Her gut wrenched, her racing heart unable to bring colour to her face or warmth to her extremities. She looked around and saw nothing.

"Calm down, my neto. Give us a full explanation, please."

"There's an ongoing court battle, my avó. Still dealing with those land-grabbers who infiltrated here all those years ago and sold forged property titles to the construction company."

"I thought that had been resolved...."

"And it was, avó, but since the state never gave you the property title, only the right to use the land, the big guys are rigging the game. They must be paying this judge really well for him to be risking his reputation like this."

"And all this on the same day as the leadership-changing ritual..." Bartyra caught her breath. "No way that's a coincidence."

"It's not, my neta. There are still people in the community, from outside of our village, who want to make money from this illegal sale, lots of people in the back pocket of those land-grabbers. They must have told the men on the other side about the death of our leader."

"Absolutely. And they struck as quickly as a snake ready to lunge," Kayky affirmed.

"But what can you do about this, Kayky?" Bartyra, already recovered, knew what the consequences of the court decision would be.

"My kin and I are already trying to get the injunction overturned in court, but we'll get buried in bureaucracy, so who knows how long that will take… Velásquez & Andrade will try to take you out of here by force! A few kin with connections among those people have already informed us that since yesterday there's been unusual movement around the ports…weapons, outside support… They're preparing an attack, my avó."

"It's not the first time, and it won't be the last, my neto." Anahy gave a half-smile; the realisation brought her more sadness than pride. "Thank you for the warning. Now hurry back over there."

"Are you sure, my grandmother? I can stay here to help…."

"The best help you can give us is fighting together with your kin to overturn the injunction in court."

"Got it. We'll do what we can, but if things get ugly around here, let us know. You can count on us."

Anahy agreed and the three of them set off down the walkway.

"Kayky, don't forget to refuel before you go. How's the new engine going?"

"Way better than the last one, Baty. Back at the port where I dock the boat, people are always eyeing it because they're jealous. I come back at them with 'it's an indigenous thing'…." Kayky let go of his worry for a brief moment as he savoured the memory.

"We've improved the quality of our biofuel, too. Take a look over there." Bartyra pointed to the piece of land that was dry all year round, which was steadily shrinking. In the clearing, they could see two domes, slightly taller than they were, wide enough that the curves at the crowns could look like natural hills, were it not for the sets of pipes. "These are new biodigesters, and they let us generate more biofuel and more electricity as well. Combining the energy from this structure with the solar panels, we don't need the public grid anymore."

"Speaking of that, Baty, is there any way you could get more panels for me? The electric bill's been tough. This scarce rain is a perfect excuse for them to up the cost…"

"Of course, Kayky. I'd be happy to help you install them." Bartyra showed as much enthusiasm as her worry would let her.

Soon they reached a fork in the path, where they parted ways. Kayky bowed his head and the elder placed the palm of her hand on the side of his face, murmuring what they knew was a blessing. The boy hurried to the pier, while the other two continued on their way. Anahy broke the silence:

"Bartyra, is there a way to preserve Mayara's body in the labs?"

"There is, my avó. What are you thinking?"

"They want to take everything from us, even our right to mourn, our right to weep for our dead. But I won't let them do that. The ritual will proceed—if not now, then tomorrow, and if not tomorrow, then later." Bartyra agreed, affliction bearing heavy on her chest. "Oh, another thing, tell all of our kin, of all peoples and ethnicities, about what's going on here. And not just them, let the white allies know too. Everyone needs to know about this absurd injunction."

Before they arrived, they could see from a distance that all their kunhãs were standing outside of the stilt house, searching for the pair with nervous looks. They were girls and women, some of them far too young, not yet ready to face the terror that the evening would bring. Among the more experienced, some still bore scars from when, many years before, they had to show their bravery.

Before they joined the group, Bartyra slowed her pace to a halt. The elder took two steps forward and turned around.

"What now, avó? What are we going to do?"

"We'll do what we and all of our kin have always done, my neta—resist."

#

Bartyra and the other jaguar-warriors gathered in the college's entrance hall at Anahy's request. When the elder left the biotech research lab, she was walking arm and arm with Taynã, the researcher in charge of the college's administrative duties.

"My netas, you are gathered here because you are our greatest hope. All of those years of training that you underwent were not for nothing—there has not been a single generation of our people since this cycle of exploitation began that hasn't had to fight, and now, once more, we need to act. Our informant kin stationed on the other side of the river confirmed what we feared, that an attack is on the horizon. They are mercenaries, well-numbered and well-armed, and they will attack today." No one made a sound, but Anahy knew, because she knew each of the women in front of her so deeply, that the looks on their faces were ones of anguish. "We must mount our defence, and today we will fight like our oldest ancestors. Listen, you all know very well that long ago our women lost the ability, in life, to transform into yawaretê, but…"

Bartyra watched the two, connecting the dots between the new leader's words and the presence of the researcher-director in this conversation with the warriors. She knew Taynã very well, and not just from the research projects she coordinated at the college, but because she was one of the biggest enthusiasts of its exchange programs. What's more, Taynã had established the network of contacts that had allowed Bartyra to discover the world through working at other educational and research institutions, not just of indigenous peoples, like this one on the Island of Jaguars, but also at traditional institutions interested in mitigating the effects of humankind's devastation over the course of its long journey on the planet. She also knew about the researcher's lifelong project, and when Bartyra linked it to this meeting of jaguar-warriors, she couldn't contain herself.

"But Taynã found a way to transform us!"

"Bartyra, since your anxiety is preventing you from listening to me, at least hear what Taynã has to say…" Anahy scolded.

The researcher delicately unlinked her arm from Anahy's. She pulled two vials out of one of the pockets in her lab coat, one with a thick black liquid, the other orangey-red.

"What you're looking at right now are jenipapo and urucrum tinctures. But they're a bit different from the ones you're used to. A few years ago, Mayara and Anahy came to me with an idea: recover our power of metamorphosis. Well, that's not exactly what we ended up doing, but we landed on an interesting result. With the help of genetic engineering, we managed to synthesise some bioactive compounds that will help you when the time comes to fight. And all of it is here in these little bottles. We distilled these compounds in the tinctures you'll be using."

"Incredible!" Barytra's eyes gleamed. "But how does it work? By absorption, obviously… but how?"

"When you all have paint on your bodies, Baty, the compounds will activate and your muscles will respond to stimuli much more effectively. This will give you more physical vigour, more agility, and more strength as well. An enhanced ability to smell and see in dim light will also help a great deal. Now, there's just one thing… It takes a couple of hours for it to take effect, and in that time, the body's reaction is not good at all. We've been trying to minimise this, but… we're in a dire situation, aren't we?"

"Of course, Taynã. You've already done such incredible work." Anahy smiled at the researcher. "We need to put our paint on immediately, or we won't have enough time."

"Ah, the amount of tincture we have available is only enough for the few of you," Taynã added. "I'm sorry to say."

"We'll have to make do, my netas, but the invaders who make it past us will have to contend with our male warriors' bordunas and arrows."

The elder had a plan and all the warrior women knew just what it was. The area around the pier was the only safe place for the invaders to disembark, but if the warriors destroyed and barricaded it, they would force the invaders to disembark on the flanks, prompting a guerrilla fight in the swampy forest on the riverbank. Surprise attacks, small groups, preferably without the use of lethal force. This was a group of women trained in hand-to-hand combat in spite of the difficulties that moving through the rainforest can bring to those who don't have an affinity with it.

Bartyra volunteered to be the first warrior to be painted, so she was the first one to break out in a fever, severe body aches, chills, delirium. As she lay on one of the nursing stretchers, her body endured the modifications. She could feel her muscles toning without gaining mass, a profusion of smells filling her nostrils, and a confusion generated by the amplified sounds inundating her ears. Her gums stung as her teeth grew more prominent, while her fingernails hardened and changed shape. Her pupils widened, catlike, and watched the warrior women go through the same reactions, one by one, their moans and whimpers causing some apprehension in Anahy and Taynã, who were watching everything, giving the warriors whatever help they could.

As soon as they could get on their feet, still feeling some effects from the reaction, the jaguar-warriors met up with the rest of the people in the clearing. The last light of day dappled the treetops. Anahy, in the middle of the circle formed by the crowd, looked out at the worried women and men in warpaint, their children playing obliviously. Before joining the group, she had gone to the woods to ask her ancestors for help and protection. Now, in the middle of all those people, she remembered Mayara's lessons and it hit her that she'd never hear them again.

"Kunhãyawaretê warriors, we are at war. Ever since the first ship docked on the shores of this land we have been at war. Ever since the first whip cracked on the backs of our grandfathers and our grandmothers, we have been at war. And now, once again, we are called to fight for our ancestral rights. They've tried every means possible to wipe us out, but we're still here. Because that's what we do: we resist. They will never understand that we and our land are one. That the same way our energy, our nourishment, our sustenance, our culture come from it, all of our efforts and gratitude emanate back to it. Come nightfall, they will try to push us out, they will try to break this sacred link between us and the ground we walk on. But that will be their mistake. Because they don't know that the night is our ally, that it is the Mother Jaguar who rules the darkness, and that these trees are all our ancestors. Kunhãyawaretê warriors, today we will once again defend our land, our culture, and our people. Today we will fight. Fight and win."

The shouts of the Kunhãyawaretê people echoed throughout the island. Anahy took the lead in the war dance ritual. The women warriors of the village formed the inner circle around their leader, arm in arm, spinning and chanting in response to the rallying calls. Immediately behind them, gathered in a circle surrounding the first, the men beat their bordunas—traditional war clubs—on the ground, punctuating the singing and giving a rhythm to the dance, rotating in opposition to the women.

The youngest and the oldest of them took care of gathering food, water, and other provisions. Everybody who was not fit to fight would take cover between the trees' colossal roots in the heart of the island, in the Forest of Spirits, where the dense tangle of forest canopies made it impossible to invade from above. Others would accompany Taynã in the infirmary, caring for the wounded. The rest of the island's residents, already alerted of what was to come, fled in crowded boats, crossing the river towards the megalopolis or the other islands—wherever they could find shelter.

At the end of the ritual, their spirits high, all of the painted and adorned bodies followed the motions to arm their defence. Anahy spoke with everyone, group by group, going over the plan to retaliate the enemy invasion. If the invaders made it past the first barrier of jaguar-warriors, the skilled archers would spring into action, and the last line of defence was the warriors armed with bordunas—those led by Ybyrajara, a strong and experienced spearman. That would have to be enough.

Bartyra and the other jaguar-warriors were wearing skin-tight black suits made from material harvested from the island's rubber trees, enhanced by nanoclay compounds manufactured in the college's laboratories, that would protect their bodies and render them undetectable to thermal cameras. They tested their communication devices and continued to adjust to their new abilities. Anahy approached them:

"We are a warrior people, just like many of our kin. But we don't fight because we want to, we fight because we have to, and it is on the battlefield that we prove our worth to the Mother Jaguar and to our avós alongside her. But it is also on the battlefield where we understand the value of standing together. Take care of yourselves, take care of your sisters, and let the spirits of the forest guide each of your steps."

Anahy searched Bartyra's catlike eyes and in them saw fear and anxiety, but behind that she also saw love. Love for what she was defending, love for herself and who she stood with. Knowing that love was the fuel for courage, the elder felt peace in her heart. With a nod and a smile she conveyed the confidence the girl needed to face the evil that was about to befall the warriors.

A few minutes past midnight, one of the urubu-drones, which had all charged their batteries in the morning's sun to ensure their reliability for night-time flight, sounded off a signal. Bartyra began to see on her wristband what the mechatronic animal had registered: five large speedboats, each loaded with equipment and twenty armed men. They were preparing to leave from a private dock on Belém's waterfront. The girl locked the drone in on the targets and directed the others towards the location.

The boats took off, and in just a few minutes they would be across the river. Bartyra informed Anahy, who was already in the Forest of Spirits, joined by the warriors who would form the last line of protection for those taking shelter there. The elder ordered that all the lights on the island be switched off. Only the truly essential equipment would stay on, as would the infirmary at the college. The Island of Jaguars plunged into the darkness, where the Mother Jaguar reigns.

The speedboats, although they were powerful, had muffled motors and glided over the river with their lights off. Were it not for the enhanced sight that the tincture had given them and the urubudrones' night vision lenses, Bartyra and the other warrior women would never have noticed them approaching. As predicted, the invaders had to disembark on the sides of the dock, on swampy terrain that impeded their movement. The green lights from their crosshairs were the only things that illuminated their path—they intended to catch the inhabitants of the island by surprise. Silently perched on the trees' highest branches, the jaguar-warriors stayed hidden, waiting for the right moment to attack. They were watched by the few nocturnal creatures that, intrigued by the commotion, hadn't fled the area. And the moment didn't take long to arrive.

One of the mercenaries tripped on the roots and fell to the ground. Once he pulled himself together, he raised his gun's crosshairs and hardly had time to notice the pair of glowing eyes staring him down. Bartyra attacked him with a swift movement, her clawlike nails lacerating the man's face, as he fired more out of reflex than any conviction that he would hit his attacker. The shots drew everyone's attention, and they all started to fire in the same direction. Then the kunhãyawaretê rained down on them—as quick, precise, and powerful as jaguars on their prey.

Despite being outnumbered, the warriors took advantage of their heightened agility to confuse and strike down the invaders. They jumped above them, attacked their faces and arms, incapacitating some, killing those who gave them no choice. They stole their rifles, hanging them from the trees' high branches or casting them into the river. And so they managed to effectively control the militia's advances.

The tactic devised by Anahy, who kept watch over the action by following the sound and the urubudrones' viewfinders, had worked. But it was too early to celebrate. Searchlights flooded from the speedboats, which disoriented the warriors by temporarily blinding them, making them easier targets for the shots from the mercenaries who seemed to be retreating. Bartyra, her sight restored, watched their movement with bemusement—until a long hiss sounded out amidst the gunfire and shouting. Then came the first bang that shook the earth.

An incendiary bomb exploded at the front of the militiamen's line of attack, and others soon followed. Bartyra saw some of the warriors get struck head-on, and not even the flameproof technology of their suits could save them. Others, close to the site of the explosion, were hit by the shock wave and sent flying metres away, along with some of the mercenaries who hadn't had time to retreat and some of the animals that had refused to flee.

The warrior women who had not yet succumbed to the shots or explosions fought bravely and inflicted casualties on the invaders. But, without the element of surprise they had earlier, they were less effective, and the weaponry they were up against was too heavy.

Then Bartyra had an idea. By the time the mercenaries noticed some of the urubudrones approaching them at full speed, it was already too late. The mechatronic animals crashed into the speedboats, piercing their hulls, breaking searchlights and other equipment, and knocking some of the men into the river.

The bombs stopped falling, and Bartyra and the others gathered the wounded kunhãs, retreating with the agility that adrenaline was pumping into their bodies. They were cornered, hiding between the trees' roots and rethinking the strategy they would adopt going forward. The jaguar-warrior glanced at her wristband and noticed that one of the remaining urubudrones was flagging a speedboat that had escaped the attack unscathed with several militiamen; it was relocating to another part of the island, towards a river inlet that would bring them dangerously close to the Forest of Spirits.

"My avó, they're heading to the Igarapé do Yby-tu waterway, they're getting close to you," warned Bartyra, who soon heard the elder's voice in her left ear: "Take your wounded sisters to safety and regroup. Get over here, all of you! We need you here in the woods. Can the other warriors hear me?"

"Yes, my avó," replied Ybyrajara, commander of the warriors armed with arrows and bordunas. "Listening and awaiting your orders."

"Ybyrajara, their firepower is very strong. When they reach the clearing, send arrows at them from all sides. Force them to enter the bush again to come after you. Then, in the middle of the forest, make the bordunas sound out."

"Say no more, my avó, we'll set up a trap for them. Be careful over there!"

Bartyra and the other jaguar warriors hurried to take their wounded sisters to the college infirmary, where Taynã and her assistants attended to them.

Then they immediately set off towards the Forest of Spirits.

A few minutes later, Ybyrajara could see mercenaries arriving at the clearing. Wherever they went, the men left behind a trail of fire and destruction, so he and his warriors had to keep them from reaching the college building. Some of the militiamen took their knapsacks off their backs and activated surveillance drones, which began to circle the area.

Ybyrajara was waiting for the right time to act. The attack would come from different vantage points in the bush, where the warriors with long-range bows were at the ready. When he noticed one of the mercenaries setting up grenades to attack the college, he gave the order.

Arrows whizzed through the night sky, cascading over the heads of the militiamen. Even if most of them didn't cause grave injuries, just a scratch was enough to incapacitate the invaders, due to the frog poison that saturated the arrowheads—an innovation produced in the building the men were trying to destroy. The grenade they intended to throw exploded in the mercenary's hand; the others didn't know where to run, disoriented by the quick changes in position and the persistent onslaught of arrows from the warriors.

As soon as they recovered, the mercenaries began to fire back, shooting towards the bush. Their drones used thermal imaging and searchlights to identify their targets. Swift as they were, many of the bowmen succumbed to the bullets.

As the mercenaries advanced, they detonated the incendiary bombs they still had left, causing more casualties in the group of warriors. But Ybyrajara's plan was working—he'd managed to direct the invaders away from the college, forcing them deeper into the forest. As they retreated, worried about attacks from above by the jaguar-warriors, they were startled by a group of warriors charging at them, appearing on all sides, armed with their bordunas and sheer bravery. Hand-to-hand combat forced the mercenaries to abandon their rifles and resort to pistols and knives. The sacred soil of the Kunhãyawaretê was bathed in blood...and the Mother Jaguar was thirsty.

Further north, Bartyra and the other jaguar-warriors darted between the trees with the agility of their four-legged sisters. The lack of video signal on her wristband indicated that the rest of the urubu-drones had been taken down. Her heart tightened. They needed to get to the Forest of Spirits as soon as possible.

"We're coming, avó! Hang on just a bit longer, we're on our way!"

"They're already here, they're..."

The elder's voice was drowned out by the sound of gunshots and grenade explosions. The militiamen who had broken off from the first group had already entered the forest through the waterway and were making their way to the kunhãyawaretê hideout, torching everything they could with their flame-throwers.

Anahy was ready to fight alongside the children and the elderly who were in hiding. As the mercenaries grew near, she heard the wailing of her ancestors engulfed in flames. If her body perished there, her only regret would be not giving Mayara the rite of passage she deserved.

Now the bullets had found a sure course. Beside her, a few of the courageous elders who had been ineffectively shooting arrows began to topple over. She gripped the staff of her borduna and asked the forest spirits for protection.

The first shot grazed her left ear, taking out a chunk, but before a second one had the chance to sink into her flesh, the jaguar warriors pounced on the militiamen from the right with all the ferocity of those who fight to protect whom they love. Like the group battling Ybyrajara's warriors, these mercenaries had also given up their rifles and were using knives and pistols instead. The fight unfurled in hand-to-hand combat, Bartyra and the other warriors attacking the militiamen with all the battle techniques Anahy had taught them. But the brutal physical confrontation was starting to take its toll. Fatigue began to set in, the warriors' movements not so agile. One by one, the Kunhãyawaretê began to fall.

Bartyra still managed to overcome two opponents with fatal blows to the neck, but she miscalculated her leap in trying to surprise a third and fell on her side. Before she could react, the man fired, hitting her in the stomach. The jaguar-warrior roared, the pain of her torn flesh compounding the weariness of her body. He approached, pistol in hand, as Bartyra crawled back on her elbows, leaving a trail of blood on the earth beneath her.

"You bitch! Who do you think you are? All this for what? To stay on this shitty island living like a bunch of animals?"

He fired one, two, three shots at her feet, just for the fun of it.

"Look around you... We're going to wipe this whole fucking thing out, burn this whole island, knock all these trees to the ground. And now you're going to die, just like all these other bit—"

Bartyra closed her eyes, waiting for the impact, but instead she felt a hot gust passing over her body. When she opened them again, she stared at the man in front of her. Canines sinking into his face, claws digging into his writhing flesh. The mercenary collapsed; he only had time for one last spasm before he was silenced forever. The animal gave its prey a shake to make sure it was dead, then dropped it. A lift of the head and Bartyra was pierced by black-and-yellow eyes. A muzzle, splattered with blood, opened into a roar that seemed to suspend, in reverence, every living thing in that place. Then they began to emerge from all sides. Agile, elegant, deadly. Dozens of them, spotted, black, brown. One by one the militiamen crumbled before the power of the teeth and claws of those animals that moved as the wind.

Bartyra turned to face her saviour. The jaguar, curious, stepped towards her slowly. She smelled the warrior's face, licked her wound, and left. The others went along with her. Bartyra looked around, confused: she had never seen so many of them. Then her vision blurred. She had just enough time to catch a glimpse of Anahy's face before losing her sight entirely. She surrendered to the darkness.

When she came to, she immediately knew where she was. Though she hadn't been to this particular room often, she knew she was at the college. On the stretchers next to her, several of her comrades in arms. She got up carefully, the wound in her stomach still aching. She used the IV stand to which she was attached as support for the painful walk. After passing through doors and corridors, she reached the building's entrance hall.

"What are you doing here, my neta? You should still be resting."

Anahy was speaking with Taynã, who rushed over to prop Bartyra up by the arm. They were joined by two other kin she didn't know, but she could tell by the way they were dressed that they were caciques of other peoples.

"What's going on, my avó?" Bartyra sat down on one of the benches, assisted by Taynã. Anahy went over to her.

"Bartyra, you've lost so much blood, you shouldn't be here," Anahy fussed. "But since I know you won't listen to me, I'd like to introduce you to Natã Munduruku and Kauã Guajajara. Their people came down the river to stand by us, my neta. They heard your message. And more kin are coming." The men waved from afar to the girl, who returned the greeting.

As Bartyra became more aware of what was happening around her, she saw several more unfamiliar kinspeople arranging mats, hammocks, rucksacks, and tote bags. The college had been transformed into a large hostel to accommodate them.

"How long have I been here?"

"A few hours, Baty," Taynã reassured her. "You were lucky—the bullet didn't hit anything inside you. Mother Jaguar saved you. Unfortunately not everyone had the same luck."

"What about the invasion? What happened? Did we...?"

"Yes, my neta, we won. Any invaders who didn't die are locked up or recovering in a guarded room in this building." Anahy held out her arm to the girl. "Since you're already here, how about you try to walk a little more?"

Taynã helped Bartyra to her feet. The wounded warrior staggered to the building's front door, held up by the two women. Outside, a crowd of kinspeople was helping to clean the mess left by the events of the night before. Smoke could still be seen in the sky as the wind pushed it further away. The burnt trees were silent witnesses to the destruction. The community would take a long time to recover, but the outside help offered by kin from all over would speed up the process. From afar, Bartyra spotted Kayky talking to a TV crew.

"Did the court order get dropped, my avó?"

"No. Not yet. But now the whole country is going to know what happened here. It's just a matter of time. They wouldn't dare try this again. Not now."

"And Ybyrajara? Where is he?"

The women's silence was enough for Bartyra to understand that the warrior hadn't fared as well as she had. They watched over the proceedings with the sorrow that comes with knowing every victory comes at a cost—and this one in particular had a high cost indeed.

"But it's time for you to rest now, Baty," Taynã said, stroking her arm. "Like Anahy said, you've lost a ton of blood. Now that it's all over, what you need is rest."

"It's never over, Taynã. As long as we live on this land, as long as their greed goes unchecked, it will never be over." Bartyra's words carried more regret than rage.

"You're right, my granddaughter. But remember that we are all one with the land, and the land is one with us. If we're sick, the land is sick too. You have to be healthy to defend the ground you walk on. Not to mention you have a rite of passage to perform. Take care, get back to bed."

"But, avó—we're still going ahead with the ritual?"

"Bartyra, if we don't keep upholding our culture, the things that unite us and make us the people we are—people who fight and resist—soon they won't even need a gun to destroy us."

"Did you see what I saw in the woods, avó?"

"I did, my neta. They are our sisters, here long before us, they are part of this earth too, they can tell who is kin and who has bad intentions, who brings evil and destruction to the forest." Anahy smiled at her kunhã. "Now go rest—we need a strong warrior to build all this anew, yet again."

For a moment, Bartyra saw a glimmer of Mayara in Anahy's expression. And she understood that the elder who stood before her wasn't just Anahy. She was all of the kunhãyawaretê who had bravely fought and resisted, for centuries and centuries, the destruction and colonisation of their people. With Taynã's help, she obeyed her elders. She went back to her room, lay down on her stretcher, and before long was dreaming of the sound of that roar and the colour of those eyes that she would never forget.

Translator's Note

The Puruborá, which translates to 'people who transform into jaguars', are an indigenous group located on the land that is now known as the Brazilian state of Rodônia (in the northwest, south of Amazonas and sharing a border with Bolivia). At one point erroneously designated as extinct by the National Indian Foundation (FUNAI), there are currently 243 living Puruborá individuals, according to data from 2014.

A key figure in maintaining the Puruborá's identity and autonomy was the matriarch Dona Emília Nunes de Oliveira Puruborá, who founded the village of Aperoi, a rallying place for the Puruborá after dispersion prompted by colonisation and discrimination led to her expulsion from her own land and FUNAI's false classification. Today it is the group's primary location, although other Puruborá are scattered throughout the state of Rodônia. D. Emília also hosted the first Assembly of the Puruborá People in her home in 2001, an important event that solidified the people's presence. As is the case with the Kunhãyawaretê, the Puruborá's traditional land is not recognised or demarcated by the Brazilian government. After she passed away in 2013, her daughter Hosana Puruborá took over as leader, a matrilineage paralleled in Moraes's story. Many other customs depicted in the story, from the war dance ritual to the jaguar-like face paint, continue to be practised by the Puruborá.

Moraes's Island of Jaguars, however, lies on the other side of the country: the Baía do Guajará (Guajará Bay) mentioned in the story is part of the north-eastern state of Pará, adjacent to the city of Belém. By setting the story here, Moraes connects his fictionalised Kunhãyawaretê with two of Brazil's largest indigenous groups: the Munduruku and the Guajajara, respectively located in Pará and its neighbouring state of Maranhão. The geographical connection allows these larger groups to come to the Island's aid at the story's end and potentially creates a link between the protagonists and the activist group Guardiões da Floresta (Guardians of the Forest). Its 120 members are dedicated to defending the 413,000 hectares of Arariboia land—which comprises the Guajajara, Awá-Guajá, and Awá people—from environmental crimes. While the group was formally established in 2013, its leader, Olimpio Guajajara, has clarified that the Guajajara people have been dedicated to their mission since the first Portuguese colonists arrived in 1500.

The group entered the international spotlight in November 2019, when 26-year-old Paulo Paulino Guajajara was brutally murdered by illegal, heavily-armed loggers. Both suspects remain at large. According to reporting by Greenpeace Brazil, Paulino's approach to environmental advocacy reflected the values of the characters of Bartyra and Taynã—he attended workshops to learn how to use technology to monitor and protect the land. As of 2020, 49 Guajajara have been killed in armed combat with loggers. The Guardians fight in opposition not only to these loggers, but also to police and politicians who prioritise exploiting the land over protecting its people.

Under the far-right populist regime of Jair Bolsonaro and multinational corporate interests, the Amazon Rainforest and Brazil's indigenous peoples are at greater risk than ever. If any group of people has the capability to counteract the destruction that colonisation and capitalism have wrought on the planet, it is those who have held stewardship of the land since the beginning—who, like Bartyra and Taynã, know how to harmonise the latest technologies with the earth's natural sustaining force. Moraes, himself from Amazônia, presents through the Kunhãyawaretê a vision of Brazil's future that is anticolonial, indigenous-led, spiritual, feminist, and, despite seemingly insurmountable hardships, profoundly hopeful.

Notes on some translation choices
"Mother of the Waters" appears as "Mãe d'água" in the Portuguese text—a term generally recognised as synonymous with Iara, a folkloric mermaid of indigenous origin who is said to live in the Amazon River. To mitigate any significance lost by the anglicisation, and to root the reference in its historical context (as "Mãe d'água" does in the Portuguese), I included "Iara" even though Moraes did not. To allow English readers to understand linguistic and cultural particularities, I endeavoured to keep some Tupi and Portuguese words visible in the text. In these instances, I provided glosses, intended to be as unobtrusive as possible, wherever Moraes hadn't already.

Sources
Libardi, Manuella. "Amazon Heroes Who Don't Give Up." *openDemocracy*, 16 September 2020. https://www.opendemocracy.net/en/democraciaabierta/guardians-of-the-forest-heroes-who-dont-give-up/.
Marçal, Carol. "The Life and Death of the Guajajara." *Greenpeace*, 8 November 2019. https://www.

greenpeace.org/international/story/26403/the-life-and-death-of-the-guajajara/.

"Morre Dona Emília, matriarca do povo Puruborá (RO)." *Conselho Indigenista Missionário*, 5 April 2022. https://cimi.org.br/2013/04/34590/.

"Puruborá." *Povos Indígenas do Brasil*. Accessed 15 May 2022. https://pib.socioambiental.org/en/Povo:Puruborá.

Illustration by Nicole Maione

Letters to My Mother

by Chinelo Onwualu

Chinelo Onwualu is co-editor of *Anathema: Spec from the Margins*. Her short stories have been featured in *Slate.com*, *Uncanny*, Apex and *Strange Horizons* as well as in several anthologies including the Locus Award-winning *New Suns: Original Speculative Fiction from People of Colour*, *The Saga Anthology of Science Fiction 2020* and 2021's *Best of World SF Vol.1*. She's been nominated for the British Science Fiction Awards, the Nommo Awards for African Speculative Fiction, and the Short Story Day Africa Award. You can find her on her website at: www.chineloonwualu. com or follow her on Twitter @chineloonwualu.

The day I found her journal, I wasn't even supposed to be on archive duty. My podmate, Afara, wanted one more day to recover from the naming celebration of the Homestead's latest baby and I was happy to take her place. It was a few days before the next harvest anyway and the forest would be all the sweeter for my return.

I had read that in the old world, people were confined to a single occupation, forced to choose one thing to which they would dedicate all their time and energy. My people would shudder at the idea. In our Homestead, we all engaged in many different activities, according to our interest and capacity, to keep the community running. But I would have loved to spend my every waking moment in our forest garden. Too many days indoors and I would long to return to its green embrace.

Our archives were the Homestead's record of itself—collections of personal diaries, notes, and stories stretching back to the old world. Each resident was encouraged to chronicle their thoughts and daily lives for eventual inclusion in the archive when they passed on. I was one of the few who didn't. I preferred my legacy to be in the vast forest garden I helped tend. In the constant genetic tweaking I did to make sure each food, fuel, and medicinal plant was its healthiest version. My records would be the folders of observational data that I kept on the ecosystem on which we depended.

Though I could stay an archivist for long, I enjoyed the smooth activity of handling books. Finding a volume's proper place on a shelf gave me the same satisfaction as discovering just the right mix of mulch for a new strain of cassava or locust bean. Perhaps it was because I was not used to handling the oldest texts that the journal stood out to me. I'm sure a more experienced archivist would have passed it by. The volume dated to the earliest days of the Homestead—just after the end of the climate wars. Normally, these records had the drifting weightlessness of shedding leaves, but this one was heavy—a clod of dirt rich with life and memory. It had a simple fibre cover, worn smooth by years of careful handling, and was tied shut with a roll of string. I was drawn to it immediately. After my shift ended, I asked to take it home.

As I made my way to my quarters, the book heavy under my arm, I took in—as I always did—the marvel that was my Homestead. Each community was uniquely suited to its environment—whether it was in the deserts of the north, or the mountain cliffs of the west. Ours was nestled in the heart of an island in a river delta, never far from our forest. There were fruit trees and berry shrubs at every turn, and vines and creeping melons twined along walls and balconies. Even the moss underfoot was edible.

My compound was typical: five brightly painted homes arranged around a central courtyard. Each house was made of live bamboo saplings carefully pruned and bent toward each other until they formed a dome, leaving space for large windows. The walls were finished with hardpacked earth and the floors lined with smooth river stones so we were always cool in the heat. Once I was home, I brewed myself a pot of tea and fetched a plate of leftovers from the communal dinner I'd missed. Then I settled into a nook by one of the windows and started reading.

The entries were undated—mostly dry, impersonal recountings of daily events. I soon grew bored, wondering what had drawn me to the volume. I was ready to set it aside when I stumbled upon the letter. It was tucked behind an official entry, as if it was an afterthought. Dashed off in an irregular scrawl where the other entries were printed in a thick, even hand, it was undated and unaddressed. To me, it was a bright bloom among a field of monotone lectures.

Hi Mom,

I miss you.

I miss you so much. Right now, I'm looking at your picture and I miss your smell, your touch. I miss how you always knew something was wrong. I wish I could hear your voice—so filled with concern as it usually was. Or just get a reassuring hug—you always gave the best ones.

You weren't perfect, you had your flaws: You never really listened, never asked questions. Never seemed truly interested in what I thought or believed. You were so wrapped up in self-loathing you could barely see a future for yourself—much less one with me in it.

But your presence validated mine. Now that you're gone, I don't know how to tell you I'm sorry. I guess I'm still angry at you....

We never told each other how we really felt, and I don't understand why. Maybe we're just too alike—both of us holding that precious piece of ourselves so closely that we'd forgotten how to share.

I wish I'd paid more attention in the times when I got to see the woman you were—behind all the rage and bitterness—the sweet, loving core of you that you hid so well. Like that time we met up when I'd just moved to San Francisco. At first, it was like when we'd go on vacation when I was a kid. You were happy. Then we got into another fight and there it was: the cussing, the name-calling... I felt like a blind man who'd gotten to see for a minute only to be plunged into darkness again.

You once asked me why I left you, but you turned away so that you wouldn't have to hear the answer. Well, here's what I would have said—if you'd been listening:

I walked away because that's what I had to do to survive.

Loving you meant being crushed by the weight of your expectations. Trying to make you happy was like working to a vague, ever-shifting standard with no breaks, no bonus, and no possibility of promotion. And if I failed, I had to be on guard for the next attack.

I understand your anger. I can't imagine how resentful I would be too, if I saw my child wasting opportunities that I was denied. But I couldn't stay stuck with you anymore.

I loved you more than you could ever understand. And I never stopped wanting to please you. I just stopped trying to because it hurt too much to keep failing.

I'm afraid of where I have to go from here. I'm sitting in your old house in Bonny Island surrounded by the detritus of war, and I don't know what's waiting for me once I walk out those doors.

I hope, wherever you are, that you're proud of me. That's all I've ever wanted.

I touched the page to turn it and the pain hit me like a blow to the chest, knocking me breathless. I doubled over, dropping the book and spilling my tea all over the embroidered carpet. When it passed, I could only lay there staring at the ceiling and straining to breathe.

Some objects from the old world, the ones that still carried the anguish of those who had made use of them, were too dangerous for my people to touch. These were usually items from the drowned cities. I'd never heard of something from the archives bearing such effect.

We had been taught that the founders of the Homesteads were enlightened ones who had evolved beyond the vagaries of the egoistic self. After the climate wars, they had seen the dark fate awaiting humanity and took the bold steps necessary to avoid the extinction of our species. But the longing and grief of that short letter was unlike anything I had ever felt. Could such raw emotion truly have belonged to a founder?

I avoided touching the book after that. I returned it the next morning wrapped in cloth and hurried from the records room as if it was also to blame for what had happened.

Returning to the forest, I thought I had left the book behind. I was wrong, for something in it remained in me.

\#

Even a month later I was still in pain, though it had softened to a dull ache suffusing my whole body. Now, every movement was a desperate attempt to stay ahead of creeping exhaustion. I felt as if I was drowning in grey waters.

I stopped attending my compound's communal meals, finding the conversations too tiring. I begged off most of my other shifts within the Homestead as I had little energy for them. Only the forest still held any joy—and even that was beginning to fade.

Afara noticed first. We'd been friends since we were children. As adults, when neither of us felt the spark of sexual desire, it felt natural for us to share a home. One evening, as we sat on the verandah, she weaving a strip of undyed mkpuru cloth, and I sorting cocoyam seedlings for the upcoming planting season, she sent me a simple thought.

Obeche, your song has changed.

I am simply tired. I thought back. I pictured the ache in my bones, the heaviness of my limbs, and sent it to her.

I was indeed tired, but it did not seem that I could cure it through rest. In fact, the more I slept, the more listless I felt. My dreams were filled with the founder's voice.

Tired cannot change the song of your birth. She sent me a snatch of the praise poem my mother had composed to invite me to incarnate within her. *It is slowing.*

I reached for the song inside myself and heard it too, a drag at the end of each note that made it sound like a funeral dirge.

I think it is that book, Afara noted. We both looked at the slim volume lying on the small table between us.

Last night, against my better judgement, I'd fetched it from the archives. I was hoping to find something, anything, within it that could lift the heavy pall that had settled on me, but I was still too frightened to read it again. How quickly she had made the connection I had missed! I caught the flare of anger that erupted in me before it could form a thought that could be directed at her. But she'd already sensed the emotion.

Talk to Great-Grandmother, she suggested gently.

My people do not believe in hierarchies. Such structures lock societies down, keeping its members from true creativity and growth. Hierarchy is a form of spiritual death. Yet, there are people whose wisdom, warmth, and compassion are so respected that they become a central hub in nearly all social circles. Great-Grandmother Nya was one of them.

Afara was right, something *was* wrong with me. But I was not yet ready to speak to anyone about it—least of all her. Instead, I picked up the book and headed to the forest.

We made sure our forest garden followed the structure of a natural forest, so there was little to mark where the Homestead ended and where the verge began. We'd started by allowing a number of timber trees like iroko and sapele to grow to full size and form an over-canopy, then we planted smaller fruit trees—mango, plantain, and guava—to create under-story layers. At just above head height, nitrogen-fixing plants like moringa provided filtered shade to ground crops such as cassava, pineapple, and corn. Climbing plants such as beans, yam, pepper, and melons were allowed to twine up the trees, and herbs were encouraged to grow where they could. It was a self-sustaining system that provided a habitat for all kinds of creatures, and it required little from us beyond the occasional pruning and mulching to keep it hospitable.

Harvests were my favourite times. At any point in the year, there was something to reap from the forest. This meant there was always plenty of food for the Homestead. Today, we were gathering the jussura berries. Of all the harvests, this one brought me a special joy.

The small, grape-like beans grew in bunches near the palm's canopy, but because its trunk was too pliant to bear much weight, our tradition was to allow the Homestead's smaller children to climb the trees and pick them. Normally, it made my heart sing to hear their laughter echoing from high above me. But this evening, my steps were dogged by a heaviness I could not name.

I sat by a small creek and brought out the journal. I began thumbing through it, but there were no more letters. The entries continued in their dry, life-less manner until the last page. I was about to close the tome in frustration when I noticed several of the volume's final pages had been ripped out. I reached to touch the series of ragged page edges, and hesitated. Even before making contact, I could feel those missing slots throbbing like an open wound.

I placed my hand on it anyway.

We're standing side by side on one of the lesser-known San Francisco piers—7 or 14, I can't remember now. I don't know it yet, but it'll be the last time I see you before the world ends. You've turned your face to the water.

Your head is uncharacteristically bare, not sure what you did with your headtie, and your short-cropped hair is exposed to the elements. When did you cut your hair? Sure, after decades of meticulous straightening it had started to fall out in clumps, but I'd assumed you'd rather wear wigs. I guess there was a lot I never understood about you. Maybe that's the fate of all children, that they can never really know their parents even after a lifetime.

You've just told me a story about the only man who ever hit you. In the middle of the night to end a heated argument, he'd slapped you across the face. You laugh as you recall how he fled after you warned him not to ever fall asleep in your presence because you would kill him.

I loved that fierce and uncompromising side of you. But it was also what made you so stubborn. Once you'd picked a direction, nothing could change your course—even if it meant you'd crash on the rocks. How many times did I come out to you? Each time it was a fight. To you, it was a decision I'd made to anger you, like my preference for black velvet clothes and silver piercings. To me, it was a vital part of myself that I longed to share with you so that you could see me for who I really was, not the girl you insisted I should be.

I want to touch you. But I'm afraid it would spark another misunderstanding. So we stand side-by side, watching the blue-grey waters of the San Francisco Bay, locked in our own thoughts. That's when you tell me the story of my conception. Of the man who raped you and would have insisted on marrying you if he'd found out you were pregnant. You describe how you had to leave your own mother in Enugu and flee to Bonny Island where you had me—alone and surrounded by strangers. When you're done, you turn to look at me and say the words that have been seared into my soul ever since:

"Sometimes, I wish I never had a child," you say.

Maybe it's the look on my face, because you quickly add: "But I am glad that I had you."

But it's too late. You suggest that we go and get dinner, as if that will erase what you have just done. I force a smile and agree. And with that, we tacitly decide to bury it.

The rest of the trip is a blur of light comments on soft subjects—nothing difficult, nothing real. At the end of it, you return to New Biafra. A few months later, after I've moved to Tkaronto, the corporate nation-state of Gilgamed will attempt to annex the Free Territories of California and the first battle of the Climate Wars will begin.

I will carry those words with me through the horrors of the war, past the desperate days of scrab-

bling survival, and into the fragile stability of new community as we rebuild our world. And when I eventually decide to take my own life, I know that's the last thing I will hear.

\#

I wake up in my own bed, a worried healer looming over me. I note Afara hovering behind her. They breathe sighs of relief when I struggle to sit up.

What happened? I send the thought to both of them, and the healer returns an image of myself comatose by the water. She'd found me as she foraged for mushrooms. The book was gone, likely fallen into the water when I'd lost consciousness. It didn't matter, though. Its damage was done.

You have been gone from us for three days, Afara adds, sending the full force of her distress and anguish at me.

She realises her mistake as soon as she does it.

I curl inward, unable to bear her pain on top of the dead woman's grief. Somewhere inside me, the vast maw of despair that I have been straddling for months finally yawns open and I am engulfed. Despite her apologies and entreaties, I slide back down into my bed and pull the blanket over my head. Neither she nor the healer can persuade me to rise again.

\#

That night, Great-Grandmother Nya comes to visit. I know it is her without having to lift my head. Her presence is like the light of the sun just as the day shifts from dawn to morning. She sits on the edge of the bed and places a warm hand on my head.

"Greetings, daughter." My mother speaks aloud, for she is the one person with whom I will not share my thoughts.

I want to tell her to go away, but I can't. My body feels like a metal weight anchored to the bed. I can't even answer. All I can manage is a moan. A child's lonely wail upon waking in the night. She sidles into bed with me and cradles me in her arms. And though she's small and frail, and I a grown woman in my fiftieth year, I sigh into her embrace. And then I'm weeping. Coarse sobs that wrack my frame, howling tears for myself and the women whose names I do not know.

My mother lets me cry. Her only response is a soft hum uttered every so often, a quiet understanding that I am in pain, that I need to feel it, and that I will survive it.

"Do you know that your birth song came to me while I sat underneath a tree?" she says when my tears finally subside. "That's how you got your name."

"I know." I'm surprised by the sound of my own voice, so rarely do I use it. "You've told me that story many times."

Though I can't see her face, I can feel her smile. "I don't always listen, do I?"

I shrug. My body is surprisingly lighter as if much of the heaviness that had dragged me down had flowed away with my tears.

"I am sorry I did not always give you what you needed," says my mother.

"You did your best."

"I also hurt you. Both can be true at once."

I am silent at that, and for a while she is too. She begins humming a tune, and I recognise it as my birth song. In our Homestead, every child is born to a praise poem composed while they are still in the womb. It is the first song we hear, and we commit it to memory before we ever speak our first words. The song is meant to embody both a child's current personality and their future prospects while connecting them to the long lineage of our ancestors. It is supposed to evoke our individual and collective identities.

As she sings, I listen closely for the first time. And I hear, clearer than I'd ever heard before, my mother's hopes for me, the love and care she'd poured into every aspect of my upbringing. And though we didn't always agree, I realise that I had never doubted that she wanted me. I think about the old world and what it might have meant to have what one did not want and to want what one did not have.

Mother, can I ask something of you? My mother has the grace not to let her surprise at my thought show.

Anything, my love.

Can you help me plan my burial?

The open field was one of the few on our island and we kept it clear for ceremonies and celebrations. A week after my mother's visit, she and I gathered everyone there. Unlike other Homesteads, we didn't have a formal amphitheatre. Instead, we had adapted the natural mounds of dirt around the space into rough terraces so that everyone who needed to sit could do so and still be able to participate in the activities at the centre of the field.

On one end of the space, a group of drum healers waited patiently. I hadn't told them exactly what they would be doing, but they had their instruments—ogenes, kolokolos, and drums of various sizes—at the ready. A massive umbrella tree growing on the other side provided necessary shade and many gathered underneath it.

For days after my mother's visit, Afara and I sat in communal meditation. I'd lanced the boil of the grief that had driven the dead woman to suicide, but I still had to heal the infection of her trauma, which still lived inside me. If I was not careful, I could spread it like a disease throughout the community. Slowly we uncovered more about her—her name, her story, and most importantly, her song.

And today, I was going to sing it.

I waited at the centre of the field until everyone had found their places and settled down. No one knew quite what I planned, and if I was being honest with myself, I barely knew either. I had chosen to wear a mixture of the green robes of a birthing ceremony, the blue of a naming celebration, and the white of a funeral. In a way, what I wanted to do would be a mixture of all three. In my arms I cradled a mahogany sapling.

My mother began the ceremony with the breaking of kola nuts and a prayer of recognition to our ancestors. Then, together, we called the woman's true name three times to awaken her spirit and her song. I started singing it and behind me, as if by an unknown cue, the drum healers began to play. I planted her tree among the grove of the ancestors. Then, I poured a libation of water mixed with milk over the plant to share her name with the ancestors.

While I worked, the whole Homestead began to take up the song. Hesitantly at first as they learned the words, then with more confidence. Only when the song was firmly upon every lip did I allow myself to dance.

As the complex polyrhythms of the drums thrummed through me, I let the song guide my steps. Each movement was a welcome and a release.

I took her pain and mine and shared it with everyone present, then I let the forest take them. Like the transformation from waste to compost her grief became a memory rich with life, a catalyst that would help me and my people grow stronger.

I danced until I collapsed. And I was lucky, for when I fell, my mother's hands were there to catch me.

Illustration by Simone Alvisini

Bittersweet Are The Waters

by Mame Bougouma Diene

Mame Bougouma Diene is a Franco -Senegalese American humanitarian with a fondness for progressive metal, tattoos and policy analysis. He is the francophone spokesperson for the African Speculative Fiction Society (http://www.africansfs.com/), the French language editor for Omenana Magazine, and a regular columnist at Strange Horizons. You can find his fiction and nonfiction work in Omenana, Galaxies SF, Edilivres, Fiyah! Truancy Magazine, EscapePod, Mythaxis and TorDotCom; and in anthologies such as *AfroSFv2; V3* (Storytime), *Myriad Lands* (Guardbridge Books), *You Left Your Biscuit Behind* (Fox Spirit Books), *This Book Ain't Nuttin to Fuck Wit* (Clash Media), *Africanfuturism* (Brittle Paper), *Dominion* (Aurelia Leo), and the upcoming *Africa Risen* (TorDotCom). He was nominated for two Nommo Awards and his debut collection *Dark Moons Rising on a Starless Nights* (Clash Books) was nominated for the 2019 Splatterpunk Award.

"Gimme eight liters of shit-water and ten packets of flavoring." Miyongi told the bartender.

"That's not enough to cover the taste Miyongi, but I'm starting to think that's just how you like it."

"Fuck off, James."

"Just saying, it's your kidneys..." He lifted two

four-liter plastic bottles on the counter "There you go. Transfer those credits and you're good."

Miyongi typed the Salamander bar's credit line into his wristband, trading a liter of fresh water for eight liters of water recycled from feces. It was the cheapest way to stretch water credits, and he needed a lot of water.

"Let me get a glass of fresh too. You owe me at least one by now."

James looked at him and nodded. "Yeah. I reckon that much."

He filled a glass and handed it to Miyongi who shot it down in one gulp. James shook his head. Most people sipped on a glass of fresh water for hours, piss-water even, but Miyongi guzzled it like moonshine then reveled in shit for weeks.

Miyongi caught his look, thinking little do you know, grabbed the jugs, adjusted his facemask, and stepped out into the evening sun.

\#

The Drought was punishment from the Nymphs.

Hiding in the clouds, they'd sealed their hearts with ice, and hadn't shed a tear for centuries. When the world was young and the oceans and riverbeds lay empty, the Nymphs cried when a child died of thirst. One day a nymph dropped from heaven and fell prey to cruel men who killed children for her tears and starved people for water, until her friends had enough, and cried their companion's misery and flooded the world.

But they had changed their minds again, watching the forests shrink and disappear, the oceans of the world shrivel to giant lakes, and the children they once mourned growing worse than their forebears. They shook their heads in the skies, refusing to shed a single tear for those people they had tried to love, and who'd broken their hearts yet again.

\#

Miyongi didn't know what to call the red fruit growing on the bush. He didn't know if they were fruit or poison yet. His grandmother had warned him about that, a few days before H2OCorp took her, when she'd handed him the old seeds and hit him upside the head so he remembered.

Everybody thought he was crazy, locked up in his apartment with some strange fetish or another, but they didn't know plants, they'd never even seen grass. Shit-water, piss-water, sweat-water, it was all the same to plants. A drop was a river, and the things that would sprout with a cup…

Things that would get him arrested for wasting water on non-humans for starts. It would cost him his entry-level job with H2OCorp, and probably his life. There's a lot of water in a human body, it would make up for what he'd squandered on plants.

He cracked the window to his cubicle and let some air into the damp room.

On the 175th floor there wasn't as much dust as nearer the ground, and outside, Amanzi spread its myriad towers for thousands of miles along the old ocean floors. From the Arctic plateau to the Atlantic Lake buried at its heart, where executives had their apartments, overlooking the sea-sized pond, where the breeze still hinted of iodine, the small waves of mermaids, and children knew the feel of water on their toes, enough of it to drown in.

Time flows the weight of water, Miyongi thought.

Now, if only we'd thought of solar panel cities before drying up the oceans....

He dumped a jug of shit-water into a large cylinder. The cloudy liquid dispersed through transparent tubes dripping over little pots and glass tanks lining the walls, and fledgling growths in early stages of germination hanging from the ceiling. Then into thicker tubes connected to baby tree stumps with ferns growing between, a lush dark green and a smell that had no name, because none of these things had any, it was just life, the sappy smell of life.

He poured the second jug into a blender and emptied the packets of artificial flavoring, watched the liquid spin purple, filtered it through a cold box into a small glass, and took a sip. James was right, it still tasted like shit.

#

Naisha stepped out of her building just as the sun sunk into the ground. In contemplation for hours, her sensitive eyes broke down every undulating ray, tentacles sliming along buildings into an orange river.

She blinked, unwrapped her blue mouthpiece and inhaled, letting the wavelets of gritty air sprinkle her tongue, rolling the dust against her palate, crushing it with her teeth. She pulled a small vial from a chain between her breasts and cracked it open, two tiny droplets of fresh water sliding down her tongue to mix with the earth and bloom within her.

The oceans within us. Worlds within worlds. She thought, tying back her mouthpiece and adjusting her goggles.

The street was an empty moat between the towers casting shadows of themselves in the glisten of a million eyes like milky cataracts. Like the ones growing slowly behind her eyes.

She ignored the thought. In the afterglow of meditation she let her feet carry her before she thought. She would see a sign and she would know. There had been a red flash, merriness and the shadow of death.

Dust rose behind her as she walked down the street, with a soft rumble turned rampage as a group of death runners squirmed past her in desiccated exhaustion, one dropping dead. Emaciated legs folding beneath her like a mantis, shredded lungs exploded in her chest pearling blood on her lips, raising small puffs of dust into already dusty air as her head hit the ground.

The others kept running, already blocks away when Naisha looked up from the corpse.

"It's mine!" a voice rang from a low-level window.

"Liar! He's a fucking liar! It's mine!" Another answered across the street.

There isn't enough water in that woman to fill a cup, she thought, as one of the runners broke away from the group and walked under the purple neon of the Salamander Bar, nearly collapsing as he pushed the doors open, and yelled.

"I'm going down drowning! Who's with me?!"

The crowd inside went nuts.

"Merriness..." Naisha said with a smile and followed him in.

"His time is nigh! Behold the great flood!"

"Behold the great flood!"

The cult of Nymphomaniacs had been the fastest growing religion for a hundred years. The torch-lit parade towards the local temple called for their messiah to bring forth the flood, and the shorter your water credits the more likely you were to be a Nymphomaniac and worship the tears of the Nymphs and the water of women. At their weekly gatherings, the Priestess would sit naked on a chair, her legs spread for the congregation to come lick the water from her fountain and quench their thirst in anticipation of the day they'd drown.

The procession drew passers-by in its wake, flowing through avenues and inundating dozens of blocks, the dusty night air awash with thousands of burning eyes and discordant voices.

Miyongi walked into pandemonium at the Salamander Bar.

"Drink! Drink! Drink! Drink!"

The patrons cheered a man sitting at the bar, drinking from a funnel James held over his mouth. He chugged for a few seconds and raised a hand to catch his breath.

The crowd roared. The man stood on his chair and yelled back at them.

Suicide by water. Nothing new. They would run miles in the dusty heat without drinking, putting stress on their kidneys, then stop at a bar and spend all their credits drinking themselves to death. Their kidneys retained more liquid than they could process, logging the blood with water and gorging their brain cells until they burst.

"How long's it been going on?" Miyongi asked a guy standing by the door, sipping on a green ice cone.

"Barely started. Fifteen minutes maybe. Good rhythm this guy, but he's bound to slow down. Got my money on two hours. What do you think?"

"I think he's holding up my beer."

"Beer huh? What you celebrating?"

Miyongi shrugged and walked away. The man was back on his chair, eyes red with fatigue, but determined on going down drowning. The bar got to keep the body and its water, and it was a good show until the seizures started.

"What's it gonna be my man?" James asked cheerfully "Moving up to sweat-water? Just kidding. Lucky day, everybody gets a free cup on the house. Don't say I've never done anything for you."

"Make it a beer for me J."

James whistled. "I'll be drowned. You're not getting that on the house. Grab a seat."

Miyongi watched the guy shooting cups down. A reddish-brown haired woman sat at the bar between him and imminent cerebral edema, and waved towards James.

She sat staring at the ongoing suicide while Miyongi stared at her, and James brought his drink.

"Here's your beer sir." James said, then turned to the woman as she turned towards Miyongi, "What's it gonna be for you, girl? You get a cup on the house on account of that guy over there."

"I'll take that." She answered, smiling at Miyongi. "Beer huh? What you celebrating?"

The beer was mostly residue from battery acid-based moonshine with a little carbonation and flavoring; it cost two liters of fresh water a glass, but he was celebrating. Nine months of crossbreeding seeds, drinking piss-water on a good day, and enhancing them with chemicals had paid off. He'd be ready to start sowing the neighborhood in a week.

He stared into her dry green eyes, her freckled yellow brown skin stretched aridly over high cheek-bones and a Nubian nose, and reached into his pocket.

"I was walking south this evening…."

"Here's your cup. Sip it slowly." James interrupted, putting her drink down.

"…and something caught my eye on the wind."

He pulled out a red flower petal before her incredulous eyes, dipped it into her glass and placed it on her cheek where it stuck softly.

"Lucky huh?"

A red flash, merriness and the shadow of death.

She caught her breath, placed her hand over his, and asked: "I live upstairs. Wanna head up?"

#

Her lanky, amber figure stepped out of the air shower, slid under the sheets, and she looked up at the small petal. Naisha was her name, and she had framed it over her bed between two small slabs of glass, the early sunrays breaking through her window lighting it in shades of claret.

"It's amazing that it came this far…" She said.

Miyongi shrugged. "It's amazing to us. Doesn't have to be." He answered, reaching for the remote and turning on the television to an ad for water insurance, shot along the beaches of the Atlantic Lake.

Running out of water credits? Spending too much on a large family? Aquainsurance is your friend in need…

"Ever been there?" she asked absently, staring at the small waves breaking on the beach.

…Water is a resource not a right. We can insure you a steady supply against a few years of your life…

"Yeah." Miyongi said, "Atlantic Branch employees of H2OCorp get to go for a day."

...*You don't want to be a water burden yourself in your old days do you? Aquainsurance: Live less, Live better.*

Aquainsurance's supply came from the water of bodies they received in exchange for a few years of fresh water. Ten years of water insurance for five years of your life, twenty years for ten. All precisely estimated. He turned off the TV.

"How was it?" she asked, "I wanted to go, but it's all my credits just the one way, and then what? Aquainsurance? Please."

Miyongi chuckled.

"It's huge," he said "But when I see that much water I stop being thirsty. It's completely lost on me...."

She punched him in the ribs.

"Seriously, it's bullshit Naisha. We need to know what we work for, and remember why we ration, remove and dehydrate people, but that's it, the day trip and it's over, meanwhile someone else is rationing your credits, and they get to walk on the beach and watch the sunset, and swim while we air shower. It's bullshit. We die, they don't, they'll cut us off one day, and it might just be a good thing, we're going nowhere in a hurry."

"You sound like a fanatic."

"I'm not a fanatic. Why? You don't believe that doomsday flood crap do you?"

"You gotta believe in something."

He got out of bed, buttoned his shirt and pants, leaned over, and kissed her.

"Then believe in me. I am the flood, you'll see... See you at the bar."

Naisha stretched under her sheets. The slither of light reflecting against the glass panel around the petal slid along the wall, the dry leaf retaining a glimmer like a pearling drop of blood about to burst. She had never thought of blood as something that could be beautiful, sharing the ephemeral tension of a flower, the intimacy of a breath.

She walked up to the panel and smashed it on the floor.

The last thing the world needed was another poet. But there she was, another troubadour facing the waterfall at the edge of the earth. She could have thrown up. But more importantly the petal was a distraction, a symbol, and you could get lost in symbols.

There were traces of Miyongi on the bed. Her heightened senses reminded her of her fading sight, and the musty smell of the man did not help her in the slightest.

She picked up her radio transmitter. The voice on the other end of the line abrupt and annoyed.

"This had better be important."

Naisha breathed in. It was.

He wasn't great as a lover, and nowhere near as tough as the aura that floated around him, but the signs had come to her and manifested. He had named himself the flood. As cynical as anything about him, but in a thousand years no one had. No one. Not in a thousand years.

Maybe it had been but post-coital bravado. Maybe he had been groomed right. Or maybe it was the last and final sign.

She looked out the window, the orange dusty air streaming like oil against the blue sky in swarms of famished locusts.

If I'm wrong....

"It is, High Priestess. We...." This was on her. "It's exactly as planned. The Nymphs will cry for us again."

\#

A group of children ran past the stone stairs leading into the temple while Miyongi walked down to the street, wiping some of the High Priestess's water from his lips, the flying nymph carved into the building behind him, her hands open invitingly, a single tear running down her cheek.

Miyongi remembered being one of those kids. Climbing the maintenance ladders up to the train tracks, licking the condensation from the freight trains hauling tanks of water, frozen in their tracks. It was common for bootleggers to hijack trains, jamming the tracks to siphon off tons of the desperate's water. *H2OCorp... How did we ever get to this?*

They got to lick condensation off a rusty train. A bounty for a thirsty child. Miyongi's tongue tingled with acrid memory.

His grandmother wasn't always easy. She was never easy. She was an absolute mess. A near constant psychobabble about salty earth and sacrifice. But she believed in those tiny dry seeds, and he hadn't betrayed that. He hadn't betrayed his word to her.

She'd never told him how many years she'd pawned off in aquainsurance to keep him alive. Perhaps that was why she was always so intense. Time was running out and she needed him to understand. Maybe some kid had licked off some of her condensation one day. Maybe she lived forever that way.

Of all his friends he was the only one who'd noticed. Despite the rust, the dry air around them, tiny, tiny things *grew* on the tanks. If anything could live on that, even ever so briefly…. His grandmother wasn't crazy, and those seeds….

He hadn't betrayed his word to her. Even as he applied for H2OCorp's Science Program. Even as he shook sweaty palms with self-sufficient predators and kissed ass. He would show those greedy weeds in their seaside towers what was what.

What was it the High Priestess said? The nymph that cried was the child who'd died? He didn't believe, but he needed all the luck he could get.

It was sowing time.

Miyongi looked around cautiously, planted a seed deep inside a crack in the concrete, and sprinkled a few drops discreetly from a canister under his shirt. The block was still empty, but the lights from windows along the towers made the dust flicker with orange waves.

The sun would rise, and the supercharged seeds would start digging roots—very long roots—eventually tapping into the Atlantic Lake and slowly turning the neighborhood green. There were plants that could withstand the drought; it would only take a few weeks.

Miyongi walked towards his building while the sun bled across the city grid, drowning neighborhoods in stifling heat. It made its way behind him, leaking through a tiny crack in the concrete where it landed on a small seed.

The rumble of a boiling kettle rose beneath Miyongi's feet and an explosion of earth and rock projected him further into the street, gritty dirt filling his mouth. He tasted blood on his tongue and rolled over on himself. The air was too thick with dust to see more than a few feet ahead, but the sound of massive jaws crunching metal to shattering glass and screams cut through the haze.

The ground shook from another direction, followed by more explosions in the surrounding city blocks, and through the swirling dust Miyongi looked up at what remained of the building behind him, and the five-hundred-foot cactus clamped to its side and growing.

#

The tide of tremors ebbed slowly. Miyongi's ears rang with the repeated explosions, but a voice made its way through shock.

"I saw him! It's him!"

A human roar whipped Miyongi to his feet in self-preservation, and he darted before the mob coalesced.

"He's getting away!"

He limped through the growing heat, turned a corner opposite from the bubbling crowd and almost impaled himself on a ten-foot thorn.

There were cacti everywhere in different stages of growth; barrel cactus like giant, prickly, green pumpkins; and more yet shooting towards the sky in spirals.

He doubled back down a side alley onto another intersection blocked by apple cacti forming hundred-foot hedges, and pear cactus, their racket-shaped leaves climbing skyscrapers, covered in gleaming red fruit.

The whole thing had gone entirely too well.

The mob closed in, blocking the street on either side of him. He fell back, crawling up against a massive green thorn, its shade darkening the crowd to rabidly gleaming eyes.

"Get him!"

Miyongi screamed the only thing sure to stop them in their tracks.

"Water! Free Water!"

They paused.

"Free water!" he pushed himself up and pulled out his knife, the crowd surged. "Wait! The plants! They're bringing water! Free water! Wait!"

He had modified the seeds to increase the water content in the pulp, and hoped the accelerated growth hadn't ruined the fruit. They should hold water, and he should filter it first, but poisoning should beat getting dismembered.

He grabbed hold of a pear cactus fruit, carving out the skin between the spines for the juicy flesh. It squished lewdly under his hand. The crowd was silent, intent on the moist sounds coming from the plant.

Miyongi ripped out a chunk and shoved it into his mouth. The juice was thicker than water and bitter, but it trickled down his throat soothingly. He carved in deeper, oblivious to the mob. The crowd rushed forward and started tearing at the fruit around him.

A gaunt, bearded man with sunburnt grey eyes, a nymph carved into his forehead, stared at Miyongi, a piece of fruit in his hand. He looked down at the pulp, pointed a finger at Miyongi and said: "His time has come! Behold the great flood!"

\#

Small pellets of plaster drizzled from the ceiling over the followers cowering in the candle-lit hall of the temple as the tremors ebbed smoothly into the ground.

The more pious devoutly drank the water that was life, assuaging all fears; their faces buried in the fountain that is all, tasting of sweet immortality and bitter, salty truth.

"So it has begun." The high priestess said, approaching Naisha as she tied a black belt around her white robes, hair like lava melting through snow.

"He did say we would see." She answered walking alongside the High Priestess.

"Indeed. What do you make of him?"

Naisha hesitated, her saliva gluing her tongue to her palate.

"Only time will tell. The Nymphs will cry or he will die, but High Priestess, he should know. He is free to throw his life away in any way he chooses, as we all are, but he was set upon this path. He didn't chose it on his own."

The High Priestess snorted. "Miyongi's grandmother was Supreme High Priestess in my day. Atlantic and Pacific. No one has held the title since. She held the last seeds and lost her mind. I thought we were done but it seems we are not. He didn't have a choice, she didn't have a choice and neither do any of us. You didn't chose to lose your eyes Naisha, yet here you are. Our lives are all drowned in the well of fate. Some sink and some swim."

She paused.

"The choice is yours, just as it was to join the cult all those years ago. If you feel you must tell him then do so, you know his temperament better than I. Maybe he will make the Nymphs cry anyway. Maybe he won't and it will all have been for nothing, but what if he turns his back and is lost to us forever? H2OCorp will hear about this, if you are right and he is it, there will be more blood than tears before we are done. Are you ready to fight? To face the consequences?"

"I'm the last person you want in a fight."

"Why? Your eyes again? We've been over this. You were trained. You'll go blind anyway. Make every bullet count… That was your commander speaking. Talk to your mother now, I'll listen… it's… it's alright."

There was but the hint of sadness in the High Priestess's voice, somewhere deep she feared she'd forgotten how to be a mother.

"I'm fine, mother… I'm afraid. Every day my vision falters. A flash and it's gone and back. I can't feel the blindness growing behind my eyes, but I wish I did, I would know, I would have something to hold on to, instead it's just this, life goes on and every day the darkness creeps closer, silently, and I… I…."

A tear ran down her cheek, the High Priestess's finger wiping it off and pressing it to her lips.

"Don't waste your waters, daughter," she said, in a rare moment of empathy. "Don't let fear consume the light, don't let the flood within you wither and dry like the rivers of old. Even when that light is gone I will be here. Even when that light is gone you will still be a priestess. There are worlds beyond sight, and they can't be uglier than this one or I will have wasted my life and should have worked for the corporations… I would have been good too. I would have been really good."

Naisha barked a small laugh. Her mother was cold. She always had been. Perhaps there had once been a fearful girl there too. Too scared to spread her legs and embrace her power. If there had she was long gone, but something remained. The piece that gave Naisha tough but tender lessons in life. The dry humor this world deserved.

"See?" She said. "That mirth will never leave you, Naisha, but before you give that boy a choice you were never given, ask yourself, when the darkness takes over, when you see the glimmer of the world that will be your last memory in light, what world do you want to see? Now come, the faithful need reassuring."

\#

Shadows of giants licked the broken buildings, draped in orange flames.

Miyongi looked up to a tower shattered at the waist, fallen into another, bridging the two buildings like an arch. Behind it collapsed structures piled into a wall, sealing off the block from the rest of the city. Everywhere concrete bloomed. Liana lassoing across streets lit in sienna spring by the flames, the giant cactus leaves swaying in waves of matching heartbeats to powerful thumps.

Beneath his feet dried blood turned slowly brown. Under the rubble bodies rotted, slowly gluing the debris together.

The survivors had cleared as many corpses as they could, and now the mountain of stone and bone piled beneath the arch, served as a platform for the Soul Extractors. Up and down the small hill they marched, distorted shadows carrying bodies up, and marching down, a transparent bag of grayish water from their dearest of dears on their backs.

Up and down for eight days now, day in and day out, thousands upon thousands.

Priestesses chanted a deep melancholy over the machines' rattle and hum. Eight days of fasting. Not a drop drunk. The priestesses' legs remained sealed, and would do so until every soul was accounted for.

It was odd how people had come together. He always thought there was only selfishness behind the layers of phony, but there wasn't, there was almost the semblance of a community here.

Miyongi watched silently as they passed. Everyone had lost someone. A loved one, a friend, an enemy. Everyone except him, he stood alone, shoved left and right, every night, and no one would spare him a glance.

He tried to help. The cult monitored everything at H2OCorp. They didn't know what to make of his little stunt. And what they couldn't understand could only be a threat. They would launch an armed foray in a few days. A few days to secure the neighborhood, grow hedges, prepare a defense, all the....

He felt a hand shaking his shoulder. He spun and looked down to an old woman, her dried, lightly wrinkled brown skin glowing eternally young under shining white hair, her light grey eyes resting gently on his face. She lifted a vial tied to a string, over his head and around his neck.

"My granddaughter's waters. Keep them. They are yours. She is yours. She didn't die for nothing. You understand?"

Miyongi didn't move, by the time he nodded she had moved on, and he was alone once again.

#

Naisha aimed her machine-gun down towards the southwest corner of the intersection from the fiftieth floor, standing on a pear cactus leaf protruding from a building.

Armored vehicles streamed up the avenue under a cloud of dust. She flashed Morse code down to the fighters behind the first hedge of apple cacti barring the avenue shut.

The world knew the neighborhood as Garden now, and it was impregnable.

#

"We got twenty tanks closing in at a half-mile!" A teenage boy yelled at a group of people lined behind the hedge.

After six months holding Garden against repeated assaults by corporate forces, they knew their job. Dozens of hands pelted seeds over the hedge and ran in the opposite direction for cover. And then it rained.

Hoses poured water from windows high above the street over the freshly landed seeds, just as the tanks rolled over them.

#

The ground trembled. Naisha watched the seeds germinate, tearing through steel hulls and bone in a geyser of bleeding metal.

The Nymphomaniacs wanted her close to Miyongi, there was a true spark in him, a rough sense of purpose that needed guidance lest it overflowed and swept them all away, but she couldn't deny the thrill of fighting for her own, and her people.

Many young girls looked into the clouds and dreamed of becoming Nymphs themselves, only a few had it in them to become priestesses. As had Miyongi's grandmother.

In those tiny moments, she felt alive again. Her sight clearer than it would ever be again, and she forgot about Miyongi, her mother, the cult. About whether he should be told why he had been given the seeds, why so much lay on his scrawny shoulders. That he was alive to die. None of it mattered. She was one with the tide, one with the hail, one with the storm.

A stampede rang from the surrounding blocks as hundreds of ground troops attempted an invasion. She narrowed her sights on them, and started mowing.

#

Miyongi heard the machine guns rattle, and stormed towards the temple.

The cult had unleashed a torrent of apocalyptic fervor through the old ocean bottoms, and stockpiled enough artillery to give them an edge, but they wouldn't last. Radios relayed messages of Nymphomaniac uprisings as far as the Pacific Lake; the Atlantic urban sprawl was a riotous wreck, and the Nymphs had yet to shed a single tear.

Soft moaning seeped from where priestesses administered the faithful; children hopped from thick leaves to their windows and back; laundry left to dry from vines over the streets leaked to the ground into furrows irrigating small gardens.

The cacti drew water steadily through their roots. The ground wasn't damp yet, but it would be. He grew fruits and vegetables; there were flowers, and people tasted something other than recombinant protein bars and powdered carbohydrates.

The High Priestesses knew he was no messiah. They had their own agenda, but what was his? He hadn't thought beyond a practical joke. He was a rebel, not a revolutionary. He'd wanted to inspire, a droplet of ether to sprinkle their dreams with.

He wasn't bringing a flood; he was draining one

hole into another. The Atlantic Lake was migrating north, and outside the hedge walls of Garden thousands were dying, cramming at the edges, hoping the walls would crack like a ruptured dam and getting hailed with bullets for their faith.

Miyongi knew what happened to false prophets, and saw it in too many eyes, staring into the dry, cirrus speckled skies and draining at his soul.

Tens of thousands had died when his fairy-tale cacti sprouted. He'd quelled their anger by quenching their thirst, but there's no such thing as eternal gratitude.

When the ammunition ran out, before the buildings sunk in quicksand, before the tanks poured in, they would turn on him.

\#

A dozen priestesses had gathered to consider strategies. Nymphomaniacs in Pacific City had secured the administration's weapon caches, but were reluctant to charge.

"We need to take the fight beyond the hedges!" Miyongi said, addressing the High Priestess. "What're you waiting for? You know how many people are trying to get in. I'm a dead man anyway, people who could barely afford a drink every other day want me dead. How many followers are you willing to sacrifice? How many priestesses?"

"Every woman's a priestess, Miyongi." She responded softly, "There are billions of priestesses. The water of women are the bitter tears of the Nymphs. One and same. Both true. Do you remember what I told you?"

"Yes." He said cautiously, "The Nymphs that cry are the dying children."

She nodded. "Precisely, but not just the children Miyongi. The Nymphs need inspiration, their faith in us restored. There have been few great souls since the Drought, you might be one of them."

He pinched his nose bone. "What on god's brown earth…"

"You're not the Messiah," she interrupted, "We've always known that. There is no such thing as a messiah, Miyongi, only the rare alignment of circumstance and an individual. For what it's worth, you are that person now."

Nymphomaniacs were insane, but it was contagious.

"So we agree?" He asked, "We're taking the fight to the company. Yes?"

The priestesses looked him in the eye and nodded.

"Great!" Miyongi started. "We have enough tanks to…."

"You must go alone." The High Priestess interjected. "Guns don't inspire. Heart does. Pour your heart's waters for us, and we'll fight for you."

He shook his head. "You want me dead too, huh? Amazing how it works…."

The High Priestess's blue-brown eyes glistened. She shook her head, walked up to him, and rested her hand on his cheek.

"You can lead the charge and you'll die anyway, if that's what you wish. But we can't protect you much longer. We don't want you dead Miyongi. We want you to shine, then to die, and then… we want you to cry."

#

Miyongi walked onto the roof and shut the door behind himself. The night was moonless, but far away the city bathed in reddish flames. He couldn't hear the screams, there'd be enough of those come morning. H2OCorp was ready to throw everything at them. The whole world would burn.

Naisha would be waiting at the bar, but he wasn't quite ready yet.

He juggled a few seeds. Tiny things, as big to him as he was to the continental plateaus, but when they burst the ground trembled. If the Nymphs hadn't cried for every dehydrated corpse in a thousand years they wouldn't cry for him; but he had one surprise left. A big one. They wouldn't cry, but they will laugh.

"Ha!" James exclaimed, a disheveled Miyongi walking into the Salamander Bar. "The asshole who killed my business. Come here and let me throw some water in your stupid face."

"Your business was never that good anyway." he said, pulling a chair at the bar next to Naisha.

"Everything alright?" she asked, concern written over the scars she had earned leading squadrons of Nymphomaniacs.

How could he have made up his mind before looking at her?

"I guess...." He said, as James handed him a glass of real beer. Real alcohol tasted oddly light, but it was smooth and refreshing.

"What did the High Priestesses want with you?" Naisha insisted.

"They don't want anything with me. They want me gone."

"Yeah, well so does half of Garden." James said. "You killed a lot of people, brother. I mean, you did help us out a bunch, but...."

"Shut up, James." Naisha snapped. "What do you mean, gone?"

He drew a deep gulp. "I'm not quite sure, a bunch of mystical nonsense but… well, either I let Garden tear me apart, or I go out with a blast."

Naisha grabbed his hand, confession on her lips but said instead: "You can save this place Miyongi."

"I don't know anymore, not a tear has fallen. We're barely holding on. I was stupid and callous. H2OCorp won't relent. The Pacific City Nymphomaniacs won't budge unless they see a sign. I'm a dead man walking and…"

"You're gonna fold to those nutters?" James asked. "They've got their finger on the pulse alright, but you can't kill yourself Miyongi."

"That's the funny part, they make death sound like immortality." Miyongi answered.

"They're just using you. You're less valuable to them alive, is all."

"I'm not valuable to anybody alive. Not anymore, maybe I should have kept the seeds to myself and let this damned place dry up and shrivel, but I had a promise to keep." He finished his drink. "And I kept it. Better people than me have died for this." He touched the vial of the little girl's water tucked under his shirt. "Too many people, and they never had a say. They're right. If I'm gonna fight, I'll fight till the end."

"You're crazier than the Nymphomaniacs…" James said.

"Or perhaps he's just a better man than you," Naisha said.

"Perhaps, but I'll be alive to tell otherwise," James said, turning his eyes away and moving to sweep the bar.

Naisha kissed Miyongi on the cheek, her eyes locked on his with an intensity he hadn't seen in the most fervent of priestesses.

"You'll bring the flood, love. You will." She said. "Come on, let's get out of here, if it's gonna be your last night then let it be mine."

"Let it be ours." Miyongi replied, to flashes of his grandmother being dragged away by uniformed thugs. He took her hand and followed her.

Miyongi held Naisha's hand as they peered through a crack in the hedges at the lines of tanks and rocket launchers on the other side. The sky yawning its darker thoughts away into a new day. More armored vehicles were lined up behind the two of them, carved with the nymph, and throughout the hundreds of blocks of Garden fanatics stood ready to rage.

"So," Naisha teased Miyongi, "Still don't believe, do you?"

"Nope, but I won't die a coward."

His grandmother had died believing in him, protecting old seeds that might have been dead themselves. It's what he would do.

He grabbed her by the shoulders, and added: "Run, run as far back as you can and don't stop, no matter what you hear. As long as you're alive, run."

Naisha's vision faltered. His face and the world blurred and exploded in vapor and resettled all at once. Something had floated in the vapor. Or had it? Was any of this real?

He deserved to know. He would do it anyway. He should know.

"Miyongi..."

What if he didn't? What if he did and nothing happened?

She had been sent on a quest but so had he. Somewhere, though fleeting their moments had slipped through their fingers, they both felt it. Tugged at each other's whim they anchored each other, but no matter what she said there would be no love. There would be no them.

Perhaps the last thing she would see was the world burning.

This had to run its course.

She breathed in and kissed him deeply. Their waters mingled and changed and they pulled away, his hand caught on her shoulder as she pushed him gently towards the hedge.

He nodded, a tear lighting the corner of his eye, and stepped through.

#

Inside the foremost H2OCorp tank, Officer Mendez's screen registered motion, a single person stepping through the hedges.

"Sarge! They're sending someone out!" Mendez relayed to his commanding officer.

"Armed?" he responded.

"No. His hands are up, he's got a small bottle, water possibly."

"Ok, this is new. Don't shoot just yet. Might be some kind of parlay."

There wasn't much to the man, tall, brown-skinned, skinny, like so many others....

"Sarge! There's things falling from his hands! He's raising the bottle over his head!"

"He has seeds! Engage! Engage!"

Twenty rockets rose, locked on Miyongi.

They haven't shot a rocket through me yet, Miyongi thought, breaking through the fruitopia of Garden into the scorching city of dusty aftertastes.

Smoke billowed from buildings in the distance; ahead of him towers stood jagged and torn, and the gleaming rows of tanks wouldn't wait very long.

He opened his hands over his head, letting the seeds run through his hair to the ground. He reached for his neck, raised the small vial of water, upturned it, and the blast of rockets rang his ears silent.

Miyongi felt a drop trickle through his hair, dislodging a seed and running from his forehead to his nose, tumbling to his lips where he caught it on his tongue, just as the seed bounced off his shoulder to the ground.

The drop dissolved against his palate. He tasted the High Priestess's waters and felt the ground tremble; smelled Naisha's neck and felt the ground shake; he felt his grandmother's arms and the ground tearing open.

The last of the droplet vanished.

The ground erupted under him.

The rockets hit home.

\#

On the mattress of a cirrus cloud overlooking the planet, fragments of ice broke from trembling eyelids to the flutter of tiny wings.

She remembered dreaming of a life of parched moments and skin stretched over bones like parchment, of mischief, of things growing, of a kiss and oblivion. She couldn't remember being before, she remembered being the dream.

Through the thin layer of clouds something rose from the ground to meet her.

Her wings sent a ripple through the atmosphere. Billions of frozen eyes cracked open, wisps of clouds drawn to each other, spiraling in circles over and around her. They stared at the impossible thing, and as the dream faded, as the tallest of the branches brushed her puff of vapor, she heard herself thinking: *Good luck cutting through a baobab you shit-water drinking....*

She giggled, a murmur echoing contagiously through the sky. Her little ribs ached, and a lonely tear rolled down her cheek and through the mist.

\#

Naisha lifted herself up; a hulking tree's roots only a few feet ahead of her, clouding her vision as far as she could see. There was no trace of Miyongi; there was no trace of most of Garden.

Dry air spun around her. She coughed, her aching lungs answered by thousands of thirsty throats.

It hasn't rained, it will never rain, Miyongi died and it will never rain. It hasn't rained....

She felt her mind melting in empty litany, when a soulectric tingle submerged her body with static, and laughter spurted around her; impossible, inappropriate laughter that poured down on her, laughed right through her, and drew her eyes upward.

A vibrating mass of clouds swirled in vortexes around the highest branches, plunging the city into shadow for the first time in millennium. The laughter turned to thunder, a rich groan that rolled brontide through the sky and exploded in anger.

A drop hit her nose.

She raised her finger toward it as another hit her forehead, then her lips. It stuck her clothes to her frame, thickened to a curtain and blanked out the world.

She turned to the armed survivors behind her, their dripping faces glued to the sky, hesitant to laugh along with the Nymphs, but ready to fight. This was the moment she had been waiting for. The moment she had trained for her whole life.

"Don't just stand there staring!" She yelled at them. "Make your way around this thing and charge!"

#

Naisha stood on a hill overlooking a gently flowing river. It wasn't a very large river, those who had rediscovered swimming could cross it in barely a few strokes, but it ran deep and it ran far.

There would be rain in the evening. Wooly nimbus clouds rolled on the horizon, streaks of virgae floating beneath, their moisture surfing ahead on the eastern winds.

But it would be hours, and the faithful waited on her to commune. They had fought hard, and millions had drowned.

Somewhere deep below the towers eroded, the train tracks rusted away in darkness, the decayed world they'd known, but they had won. They had struggled to rebuild, and what they needed now was healing. She turned to face them; hundreds of thousands with eyes only for her and her fellow priestesses. Miyongi's Tree a lone mountain rising from the Sea of Tears hundreds of miles behind them, piercing into the bluish clouds, its myriad branches twisting into and over the waves, stretching infinitely in her mind as she danced along them bathed in shadow, the clarity of day drowned away in the fault lines of her memory as her eyes milked over with the first true breaths of a new world.

She embraced the darkness and removed her white dress, letting the moist breeze humidify her naked flesh, felt her chest dampen slightly, sat on her wooden chair, covered her breasts with her hair, knocked her head back, and spread her legs.

Behold the great flood!

Illustration by Elisabetta Marconi

THE SHADOW ON THE CRYSTAL

by Gabriela Damián Miravete

translated by Robin Myers

Gabriela Damián Miravete (Mexico City, 1979) writes stories and essays. She is a professor of cinema and literature, co-founder of the art and science collective Cúmulo de Tesla and the Speculative Literary Festival in Spanish Mexicona. Her stories have been published and translated into English, Italian, French and Portuguese in volumes such as *A larger reality / A Larger Reality*, part of *The Mexicanx Initiative Scrapbook*, a finalist project of the Hugo Awards and *Three Messages and a Warning*, finalist of the World Fantasy Award. She was the winner of the James Tiptree, Jr. Award (now Otherwise Award) for "Soñarán en el Jardín", a story about a future Mexico in which femicides no longer exist. Soon her short story collection *La canción detrás de todas las cosas* will be published by the independent project Odo Ediciones. Twitter: @gabrielintica. Instagram: @miradavaga

The following information conveys, in their entirety, the contents of Item 54-936 in the archive of the Anonymous Society for the Conservation and Study of Opal Suits, or ASCSOS (sole copy). The item in question is a green hardbound notebook of 300 stitched white pages containing the field notes of Dr. Dacia Arturo during her work as an external project consultant at the Naica Mine (Saucillo, Chihuahua, Mexico; Coordinates: 27°51'03"N 105°29'47"W; UTM: 13R 451528.94150454 3081498.8821721), from June

2007 to August 2009. It encompasses her observations on the interior of the mine and its major faults, the Cave of Crystals and the Cave of Spades; it also includes maps, notes, and sketches. In addition, it contains the doctor's personal reflections and correspondence with her sister, Lucía Cocom, as well as with her colleague on the research team at Naica, Ana Otálora, PhD in physics (45 pages, printed emails affixed to the pages with adhesive pencil, newspaper clippings, and other documents).

June 27, 2007

I didn't sleep a wink last night. I was nervous. I haven't been excited about a descent in years.

As soon I took the San Francisco ramp inside, I felt a tingling in my belly, like a girl with a crush. We crossed the tunnel, rode the mine elevator down, and received the fierce heat of its breath. We paused before we stepped through the armored door. I touched the warm, transparent methacrylate panel that separated us from the enormous selenite crystals. If I wanted, they said, I could go in without a protective suit as part of a group that would linger for just six minutes in the cave, since no (human) body can handle any more unprotected exposure. I instantly said yes.

#

We crossed that threshold between the habitable and the uninhabitable. I've rarely felt so present in my own body as when I entered the Cave of Crystals. When the light from our helmets expanded everywhere, piercing the milky translucence, I thought of the pillars in the children's song about Doña Blanca. A magical kingdom. The 99% humidity had us dripping sweat, like a ghost of the water where the crystals grew submerged. Impossible for any liquid to evaporate in there.

Seeing my shadow cast onto those vast formations, twelve meters high and four meters wide (as tall as a two-story building, thick as a kapok tree), my heart began to race so hard that I nearly mistook the feeling for tachycardia when your blood pressure drops. Breathless, I thought I might cry with the sheer joy of it. Don't be ridiculous, I told myself, you can't risk getting dehydrated, can't waste a single drop of water. I knew the danger we faced: unbeknownst to us, our eyes and innards could cook inside our bodies, as if our flesh were spinning around inside a microwave. Only then did the temperature really get to me: 49 °C. I emerged reluctantly, legs trembling. I gulped down a whole bottle of water on my way back to the hotel and fell asleep as soon as I hit the pillow. Just as I'd been warned would happen, I slept for two hours straight. Of course, I dreamed of the opal suits.

In my dream I saw, as if floating above it, the entrance to the grottoes in Oxcutzab. I felt like I was crawling through the tunnel that no one had ever explored before, the same one where I heard, almost twenty years ago now, someone shouting my name beyond the rock. I entered the January Dream Cave and saw the opal shimmering on the walls, heard its echoes, and felt exactly what I'd felt then: wonder, tenderness, terror. I woke filled with melancholy. The moon was high in the sky. I couldn't get back to sleep, which is why I'm writing this.

I'll confess that I feel envious of the attention and resources granted to the Naica formations. Why is it that the opal suits, in all their splendor, haven't been given the opportunities that the gigantic selenite crystals have? Their iridescent beauty was the least of it: there were the peculiar furrows sketched into their structure by who knows what metamorphic process. There was the issue of their dating, a real puzzle. And the most extraordinary thing of all: this mineral could emit strange vibrations and sounds. Our team worked so hard to decipher what had created them, why the sound tests triggered alterations in people's consciousness, what kind of systemic purpose they could have. There was so much to study!

I think I've distanced myself from the ASCSOS because I'm only just starting to accept that the psychiatric committee, which determined that the experience of the opal suits was caused by collective psychosis, was right: it was nothing but a beautiful accident to which we ascribed an imaginary significance. In the end, I was devastated when the research project got cancelled—not because I believed that we'd lost some Message Dictated by Voices from the Beyond, but because we were left even more ignorant than before. I guess what affected me most, in truth, was realizing that human stupidity and greed are always making us lose the chance to understand the enigmas of the world.

But I'm being unfair. The Cave of Crystals is a marvel, too. They're astonishing, those selenite presences, their desire to grow patiently, tirelessly, for thousands and thousands of years. I need to remember that not every discovery has to be spectacular for us to feel an urge to protect it and understand its purpose. Earth has enough wonders as it is; there's no need to embellish them with myths.

My dream left a bitter aftertaste. I suppose I still have a lot to process. I'm grateful to be researching again for the sake of knowledge itself, after all the years I did it to finance our pipe dream of the opal suits while the mining and oil companies used my work to line their pockets.

July 9, 2007

I can't help comparing the hydrothermal source of the Naica crystals to what we thought the source of the opal suits might be. The Naica mountain range rose up when a hot spot, a serpent made of magma, climbed high enough to elevate the terrain, but not enough to form a volcano. The strength of the hot spot waned, although the nearby groundwater reserve remained practically at surface level, above a magma chamber one or two kilometers deep. Later, hundreds of thousands of years ago, the rain falling onto the earth gradually seeped down into that reserve and was enriched by scores of minerals, especially calcium sulfate. The magma chamber went about its business and heated the water, which rose up again through gaps in the rock. The water slowly cooled and the calcium sulfate was progressively diluted, while gypsum settled along the surface of the limestone rock in the specific order the temperature allowed. There was a perfect equilibrium, silent and unaltered, of flooding and temperature, of all the conditions that let it grow like a strong-limbed tree underground. And the gypsum adopted those selenite forms, mammoth and crystalline. *Doña Blanca está cubierta / de pilares de oro y plata*, goes the song. Her pillars shaped themselves, little by little, approaching each other at a distance of two hairs' width per year.

If we humans hadn't bothered them with our machines, the crystals would have fused together in a transparent embrace, shrouded in darkness, never lit by any beam. We never would have learned about their persistence and their damp, their existence at 290 meters below ground. But selenite has always known about the world above. At the very least, it harbored the pollen of the vegetation that the rain once dragged into the subsoil when this whole desert was a humid forest. And it's highly probable than inside those pillars is some minuscule scrap of skin or bone, some trace of DNA, inorganic jewels containing an organic gem, a testimony of life.

By contrast, the source of the opal suits is entirely uncertain. We know that the common opal is also formed by means of a hydrothermal process. We know it loves to fill gaps; to replace, molecule by molecule, a piece of wood, a bone, a pearl, a nautilus shell, for millions of years, with the patience of someone who has all the time in the world. But we still have no idea why the opal suits appear in such superficial layers, coexisting with rock formations in figurative infancy. How is it that such a long process, geologically speaking, can occur without any overlaps or folding in the strata? It's not just that it's been filtered into older rocks like silica in gel.

We already knew it was possible to create opal in a lab by harnessing more violent chemical reactions, forcibly accelerating a metamorphic process, thanks to the methods of Slocum and Giles, which take months or years. But these techniques shed no light on the source of the suits, either. If we couldn't figure out a geological cause, some external factor must have strengthened its transformation. In this sense, we thought the process might have been triggered by a biological agent. But what kind of microorganisms, or even fauna, could have altered its environment so drastically?

"It must be a species with alchemical talents," we jokingly concluded in the ASCSOS.

It was such an unsettling idea, both on the research team and outside it. Not to mention the commotion that ensued when people who heard the sound produced by the suits—people who were scientists, no less—responded in totally irrational, even ludicrous ways. They claimed they'd felt as if they were living in a dream, or heard voices, or thought they existed out of time. Hallucinations, really.

My own experience was confusing, but intensely emotional. Despite my scientific mentality, I can't deny that I still see and hear, when I'm asleep, the sensations that the suits etched into my consciousness with their sound. They still feel like important messages I don't know how to interpret. We couldn't get any closer to understanding them, and that unfinished business is what plunged us into this chasm of irrationality. We should have gotten to the bottom of it. Everything would be much easier if the residue of the experience didn't keep playing tricks on our minds.

Lucía used to say that it's idiotic to think the world can be hygienically isolated for analysis in Petri dishes. But how can she say this (we still object today) when "hygienic" persistence is exactly what has allowed us to attain certainties, survive epidemics, build machines that have crossed the borders of the solar system? My sister and I see the world through different lenses. To understand each other, we both need to wear the glasses of affection.

July 18, 2007

[Newspaper clipping used as a bookmark between notes in the diary. They likely correspond to June–July 2007. Excerpts have been underlined in certain passages.]

THE MINING SECTOR: OWNERS OF MEXICO'S WATER

In Mexico and around the world, information on how much water has been contracted out to mining projects, and how much these projects use, is withheld from the public. As a result, there is no way to know how much water these consortia contaminate on a daily basis. Mining companies operating in Mexico are granted the volume equivalent to what would satisfy the human right to water of approximately twelve million people. We must bear in mind that 13.8 million Mexicans have no access to water in their homes.

In this sense, the mining sector is a public health problem: the gases and substances released during the extraction and transformation of minerals have a severe impact on water, soil, and air. The Ministry of Economy is supposed to regulate these procedures, but there are no detailed reports, at the state or federal level, on the conduct of each mining company or on their water consumption. To obtain such information on the national scale, one must pay a fee of approximately seven million pesos. The same situation applies to the studies produced by the Mexican Geological Service, which are on sale to the highest bidder, starting at seventeen million pesos. In this way, entrepreneurs can easily obtain the information, while it remains virtually inaccessible to citizens and landowners. Access to public information is divided between those who can pay for it and those who cannot.

UNPUNISHED CRIMES AGAINST LAND RIGHTS ACTIVISTS

According to the Observatory of Mining Conflicts in Latin America (known in Spanish as OCMAL), sixty percent of Mexican states have documented conflicts pertaining to extractive activities. Mexico is one of the four countries in the region with the highest number of mining-related socio-environmental conflicts. The suppression of activists who oppose mining projects in indigenous communities is especially severe, as more and more people who speak out in defense of communal territories are being murdered.

My sister keeps sending me newspaper clippings. At first, she did it to keep me informed on what was happening there, because the latest events rarely appeared in newspapers or on TV. Over time, her selection took on the tone of subtle persuasion: suggesting that I'm on the wrong path, trying to show me the perversions of the companies I could end up working for, how dirty their dealings are, the damage they do to the environment and local communities. Although she knows it's impossible to conduct meticulous research that benefits multiple disciplines without company resources, she insists on pointing out the dark interests behind every investment. As if that weren't enough, she scolds me: "It's like you hadn't even been hurt already."

How dare she imply I've forgotten everything I went through? The disgrace to our work, the closed doors, the threats. I just don't get it.

What does she expect me to do? To me, working for this company means a chance at making real progress in what we know. Like it or not, they have the capital to make it happen.

It also means I finally have some financial stability and can stop freeloading. I don't understand my sister. I don't understand how thinking people, people who worry about the wellbeing of their communities, can refuse to move forward. I know that attitude very well: they'll do anything as long as they can uphold their romantic ideals. They'd give their lives for The Cause even if their families suffer from it. We've spent many sleepless nights over my sister's activism, fearing for her life. Now that kind of idealism makes me cringe. I can't deny that I did exactly the same thing when I was young, especially because I looked up to her, admired her. Plus, I was naïve. But life has forced me to learn and leave the fairytales behind. The sooner people try to adapt and let go of that cruel optimism, the kind that tricks them into believing it's even possible to change the fucked-up system in force, the better.

July 27, 2007

Sometimes I think this project, just as the opal suits were for me, is a truce offered by the world, a tiny utopian bubble: people from all over the world sharing processes, experiences, theories, even recipes. The studies are pretty interdisciplinary here. I was excited that there was a medical area. Its leaders, Kepa Ugarte (Basque) and Eusebi Noc (Catalan), study the effectiveness of different technologies on the human body. I was surprised to see an artist painting watercolors based on photos taken inside the Cave of Crystals, although I don't really know how useful they'll be. I forgot to ask her name.

What I found even more exciting was the sewing workshop. It's organized in close coordination with the medical area and it plays a key role: the harsh conditions inside the mountain called for a special suit that would make it possible to spend more time inside the caves. It even has a name: Ptolomea. It's a pair of waterproof overalls made from course fabric, and its middle layers contain ice pouches to keep the temperature cool and bring down your body heat. It has an oxygenation-based refrigeration system that lets you keep breathing fresh air, since one of the most serious problems inside the caves is the effect of the humidity and the high temperature inside the lungs. Water starts to condense in the pulmonary tissue, and the impact is like a steam cooker: internal burns on a low simmer. No one, not even those of us who live in sticky ovens like the Yucatán Peninsula, can survive it. It's not for nothing that the suit is named after Round 3 of Dante's Ninth Circle of Hell: the icy lake.

There are three, each younger than the last, like the Fates: Conchita Ortega, Alejandra Hernández, and Marisol Guevara. They were members of the seamstress union that formed after the earthquake in '85. After spending time around the rescue workers, they threw themselves into the manufacture of protective suits for navigating dangerous environments. That's why they were nicknamed, only half as a joke, the Disasters. I'm amazed by some of the ideas they've come up with. Their lab has the resources to keep experimenting with materials and designs. They're also a riot. They make fun of my Yucatecan accent (which I claim I don't have), so I mimic theirs (which has a Veracruz/Mexico City lilt).

Ana Otálora works closely with them. She's a research physicist I've run into several days in a row, just after dawn, when I take my walk in the woods. She invited me to go birdwatching on a guided tour led by a defender of the Tarahumara forests; everyone knows him around here. I'm sure he'd love Lucía and he'll hate me. Maybe I'll go.

from: Lucia Cocom Arturo
to: Dacia Arturo
date: July 29 2007 17:50
subject: Woods

I went birdwatching in the (freezing!) woods. At five-thirty in the morning, but it was worth it. We saw cardinals, parrots, hummingbirds, and even an eagle. Fabulous. The guide, Isidro, told us lots of things you would have been interested in. There's an ugly conflict around here over the poppy plantations, but people like him fight back it. It made me think of you. Take care of yourself, you moron.

August 1, 2007

The Disasters showed me the latest prototypes they made in the workshop: the first was a protective suit made by Marisol and Ana. Their goal is to keep the wearer's body temperature down for longer than Ptolomea. The new model is as delicate as a second skin, soft and gummy; it's so small that it looks like an infant's onesie, but its elasticity, and especially its resistance, is what does the trick. Ana said the eventual hope is to introduce superconductive threads into the weave that will regulate and keep temperatures low for a couple of hours, although her physicist colleagues have their doubts.

The other prototype is a pair of gloves whose material and design absorb the vibrations of heavy machinery to reduce its harmful effects on the body. The motive behind this project is a little sad: Concha's husband developed HAVS, a nervous system disorder that causes neuropathies and other terrible ailments as a consequence of having used a jackhammer his whole life, working in construction. "He was the one who taught me to sew on buttons and now he can't even do them up on his own shirt," she told me.

I'd like to be here when they test the prototypes and study how they work. The idea of protecting the body from the impact of intense vibrations is really amazing to me. I thought of how interesting it would've been to have the Disasters in the lab at Oxcutzab. Instead of working, I started to ramble: my Achilles heel.

What kind of suit could protect the wearer against violent geological events? I asked Ana, using a volcanic eruption as an example. How could it be made thinner and more comfortable than those huge aluminum outfits no one ever wears? Something with a good helmet, something that could offer protection against sulfuric gases, maybe even with footwear, for collecting more audacious lava samples… We both trailed off, thinking, until a sudden sound made her take out her recorder.

"Did you hear that?" she asked.

All I could make out was the usual birdsong, but I knew that wasn't what she meant; she'd heard something that put her on the alert. For a moment, I thought it could be the unmistakable vibration from inside the opal suits, that Ana could hear it too. The truth is, though, I could only perceive the constant buzz of the machines extracting water from the mine. Ana shook her head and we kept brainstorming ways to incorporate a helmet and gas mask into the jumpsuit they'd invented.

From then on, our imaginations have run wild whenever we're together and get to exchange ideas. We're going to suggest them to the Disasters. "I bet they'll tell us to fuck off, that it's just a castle in the air," I said to Ana, although the next day we all met up at our usual hole-in-the-wall for lunch and ended up drawing all over the napkins together.

August 10, 2007

I've been reviewing the research on the biospeleothems at Naica. Evidence shows that microorganisms controlled the processes of certain minerals in the cave, where biogenic structures have been preserved inside the deposits of nine minerals: calcite, coronadite, celestite, dolomite, fluorite, and goethite. What's more, it's been proven that they were also responsible for the formation of hectorite, detected in a cave for the first time. Penélope Boston, a magnificent researcher, ventures that there could have been over thirty new species of microorganisms surviving inside the crystals, their lives suspended for fifty million years, sustained by manganese and iron.

This has brought me back, in recent days, to the hypothesis that some life form was the metamorphic catalyst for the opal suits. I think living things must have a closer relationship to these minerals than we think. The filtration and deposit of silica gel takes thousands, hundreds of thousands of years, but the fractures in the opal suits were caused by a sudden event, an accident that set off a shockwave, cracking the inside of each specimen in a highly specific way.

We know it was a kind of unusual, high-intensity vibration, probably a sound vibration, since the opal suits are, in turn, a record of that sound. And yet that odd vibration must be shared by the different regions where specimens have been located—although maybe tricky for local residents to detect, being a subterranean event. This unknown species among the troglofauna would have to be either as tiny and numerous as ants or less numerous and much larger, like the small or medium-sized mammals of the wooded areas. They'd need to follow underground migratory patterns, which would make them even more evasive to the human gaze.

Maybe they're extremophiles that can survive in great depths, but can also venture into shallow cavities. In order to have a major impact on the morphology of the rock, its conduct would have to be synchronic, producing a kind of simultaneous stridulation, like cicadas, which make their bodies vibrate to communicate. But the frequency and intensity of those vibrations would have to be so intense that they alter the rocky environment they inhabit or shelter in. And so, of course, their bodies would have to be able to resist such displays of energy and force. Maybe they have some special covering, like the sea snail that lives in close proximity to hydrothermal ocean waters, practically chimneys, and developed a shell with iron scales. Or, speaking of scales, maybe they're like pangolins, with paws and claws that can dig swiftly into the earth. Or maybe they're insects with diamond exoskeletons. What might they eat? Shit, I don't know anything about that. There are tons of possibilities. Life is exceptionally creative. In any case, what would be the purpose of producing this vibration? What's its adaptive function? Mating? Scaring off certain predators?

I struggle to imagine the process itself: the moment when these creatures would produce the shockwave that transmutes rock into opal suits. I wonder if it's as beautiful a spectacle as starlings during *sort sol*, when they choose a place to shelter and sleep. Thousands and thousands of birds, flying as a flock, following each other in synchrony, forming huge shapes in midair that look like a single creature vast enough to darken the sky, murmuring over the swamps of Jutland in the dusky light.

But not even the murmurs of a million starlings could "shake" the rocks into forming opal suits. The hypothesis we reached in those days was, of course, totally impossible. The vibration would have to be as powerful as an earthquake. There's something in the supposition that would explain why this kind of phenomenon has never been documented: it would be difficult for a human being to survive such a wild unleashing of energy. The vibration would be so intense that it would penetrate their bone mass. Even their skeleton could be altered by it.

Enough, though. I sound like the latest quack on a TV show about cryptozoology. Been there, done that—it's like I haven't learned a thing.

[Printed emails exchanged between Arturo and Lucía Cocom. The newspaper clipping is undated.]
from: Lucia Cocom Arturo
to: Dacia Arturo
date: August 27, 2007 9:50
subject: CAREFUL
Mulixita: You mentioned your friend and the forests. This is just to show you what things are like at my end. Be careful out there, okay?

ELDERLY SHARED LAND OWNERS KIDNAPPED
The communal land owners, mostly elderly men and women, had protested in the town square in previous weeks. However, on the night of the 27th, they were rounded up by the police, blindfolded, and taken on an inexplicable 450-kilometer ride around various municipalities. "It was a mass abduction meant to intimidate us and it ended at the precinct. We were accused of attacking the road infrastructure," the farmers expressed. To be released, they were forced to sign a statement without receiving any legal counsel.

August 31, 2007
We ran into Isidro and went to lunch with him, but he'd left by the time we set out to walk in the woods for a bit. We stopped for Ana to record something and I suddenly felt dizzy. "Earthquake," I said to Ana, just as she asked me, "Do you hear that?"

It was a rumble like the kind you can hear during a quake, and at the same time it was music. It was slightly muffled, like the song at a party seeping through a closed door, but I heard it or felt it both in my ears and my feet: it was the vibration of the opal suits.

Ana immediately lay down and pressed the microphone to the earth. I placed my ear against the ground, closed my eyes, and focused. Every hair on my body stood on end with the certainty that I was hearing, right then and there, what the committee that canceled the research project had dismissed as collective psychosis, as nonexistent. I don't know how long we spent there, stretched out, our bodies receiving a sound that followed a certain pulse, a certain breath. Then the vibration came undone in a crystalline crash, like glass being pulverized. Then silence.

We got to our feet. Ana's eyes were damp. I was dry and stiff as a piece of firewood. I felt heat in the earth that my fingers still clutched.

"What was that?" Ana said, wiping her eyes.

"Have you ever heard that before?" I asked, realizing I was out of breath.

She said she'd been trailing the sound for some time now, that she was obsessed with it, and for some reason she thought I'd heard it too. I nodded. My hands trembled.

"I've heard researchers talking about it. But I'd rather you tell me."

And as we headed down the slope, as we ate, as evening fell, I told her our whole story, the story of the ASCSOS. That I was just a kid when we found the opal suits and made lots of mistakes. That we were on the verge of locating a particularly rare piece in the jigsaw puzzle of the world, something between the organic and the inorganic. That we discovered a marvel that could change our relationship with the mineral realm, with time and consciousness and so with the planet itself. That such ideas didn't sit well with the people who wanted to profit from the research. That they denounced and discredited us. That, if it weren't for the Anonymous Society for the Conservation and Study of Opal Suits, there would have been no trace of what we'd found.

September 9, 2007

Early Monday morning, Ana stopped by and said she'd told the Disasters we had to meet in secret.

"You need to tell them everything," she said. I flushed with shame, and felt a sudden flare of anger at my friend and maybe fear. I'd spoken to her in confidence! As an expression of the trust between us and nothing more; not as a way to defend the opal suits or anything of the kind. I started to protest, but I stopped when I saw the look on her face.

"What we heard yesterday—we can't let it go, Dacia. We don't have to tell them if you don't want to, but we need to do our own research," she urged.

"We can't," I said.

"Where would you say the source of the sound is?" she asked.

Dazed, I told her what I'd been speculating about: near the entrance to the third level of the mine, no less than five hundred meters deep.

"We have to go in there," she announced with a determination I never would have imagined in someone so gentle.

"But it's blocked off! We can't. And it's very dangerous."

Ana looked at me in silence. Ashamed of my cowardice, I yielded, though I wasn't convinced.

"Okay, let's tell them. But no one else," I added. In any case, she's being naïve: there's no way we're going in. That entrance is blocked off for a reason.

At two, we went to the cabin, our favorite hole-in-the wall lunch spot. It's usually pretty empty, so we could speak freely there. I had a bowl of mushroom soup, quite spicy, and a cheese quiche, but I talked so much that I took in more air than anything else. I never could have anticipated the other women's reaction when I repeated the story I'd told Ana and shared my theory about the source of the January Dream Cave. They had lots of questions, but they didn't seem to doubt anything I said, not even Ana, who shares my sense of scientific caution. Their questions struck me as crucial, actually, in a way they maybe wouldn't have twenty years ago. Marisol asked the one I can't stop thinking about: "How can you be so sure it's a species that nobody has ever seen before? Maybe people have documented it for a long time, but in other ways. Have you researched what the local people have to say? Maybe there's some truth in the legends."

I was *the local people*. I grew up there, in the presence of gigantic insects, legends about birds flying beak-up, cave ghosts who help lost spelunkers find the way out, cenote-dwelling spirits to be treated with respect. I believed in them as a child. When I was older, I understood that this belief is a way to protect sources of drinking water. And yes, some of those stories involved mysterious music. Tour guides tell dry, soulless versions about rocks that release musical notes, that *say* things. But if we wanted to conduct respectable research, turning to those beliefs wouldn't really work to our advantage. We'd limited ourselves to asking people if they'd felt the earth vibrating or shaking, since the geology of the Yucatán peninsula, characterized by its limestone, is as porous as a wedge of Gruyère cheese, and its location makes it practically devoid of earthquakes. I confessed that we discarded any answers with even a trace of superstitious or supernatural interpretations. I was ashamed to admit to the Disasters that we never paid any attention to what people had to say. Why? I felt a surge of anger at myself and went to the bathroom to wash my face.

But when I returned to the table, Alejandra had already sketched, on the back of her paper placemat, a silhouette much like the prototype of the refrigerating suit, with one new element: external reinforcement made of the vibration-proof material used for the gloves.

Conchita shook her head, thrilled, exclaiming, "There's no such thing as coincidence. Mijita, do you really think you landed in this workshop by accident? No way, dear heart. It was meant to be. There's plenty of leftover anti-shock material to experiment with."

Ana looked at me, chewing pensively on her left thumbnail.

"We could request permission to enter the third level of the mine," she said. "It's the perfect place to test this new prototype. It's easy to justify using the material. We won't do anything in secret. We'll be safer that way."

October 8, 2007

Ana pulled me aside in the common room.

"I need to show you something in the woods," she said.

Later, sitting on the ground near the spot where we'd felt the vibration, I examined the sketch. It showed part of the suit I'd flagged as problematic: the protective layer against the possible emission of toxic gases. The ideal suit I'd fantasized about had an integrated mask and a visor or shield for the eyes. In the drawing, the Disasters' solution for incorporating these elements—and making sure that the materials wouldn't be damaged by the extreme conditions—was so simple and brilliant that I laughed as it sank in.

"We have to do it," Ana said.

"What if we find your missing puzzle piece down there in the abandoned shaft?"

I recognized the look on her face: blind excitement. "I believe you, Dacia. I'd never heard anything like that."

I could feel hope, which has never left me, churning inside my belly with the nausea of fear, which hasn't left, either.

"Leave out my own experience with the opal suits and the sounds you've recorded," I answered. "Let it be part of the projects you and the Disasters were working on before I got here. Find a way. I know what I'm talking about."

Ana pressed her slender fingers into my hand and smiled. "You can count on that. But you're coming with me." And I took a deep breath, as my sister taught me, before I smiled back.

October 16, 2007

I accidentally overheard a conversation between two co-workers I only know by sight. They were talking about Ana. They criticized what they see as a "waste of resources." X wondered aloud if the leadership knew she was close to me, since I can't be trusted. According to him, I'm an ex-hippie who joined a group of pseudo-scientists in the eighties who claimed we'd heard voices in the minerals just because we took drugs. Y (I really don't know their names) said sure, maybe I'd run off the rails professionally, but at the end of the day I'd discovered a new kind of opal and mapped January Dream when I was still a student. X stayed on his high horse. He said he thought it was ridiculous to enter a part of the mine, and with equipment funded by the company to boot, where there's "nothing to exploit."

I think it's hilarious how people think the money of the company that employs them is their own. Besides, that part of the mine is in fact the right place, because it has the necessary conditions for the model suit (or at least the part that Ana defended): less ventilation, higher temperature. I find it less funny that people think monetary gain is the only reason to do research.

I knew my bad reputation could come back to haunt me. Fifteen years ago, memos with dubious government seals sent to private companies said that we, the ASCSOS, had stolen the opal suits. This wasn't entirely true: we took charge of them because no national institution was willing to incorporate them into their collection. There was a leak of specimens to foreign collectors, which we actually appreciated, seeing as how our resources barely sufficed to protect and care for the small reserve we'd rescued. Who else would ever tend to those demanding silicates, which, once out of the rock, require periodic hydration and stable temperatures to be conserved without alterations, like plants? Only us.

This confirms that we were right to propose the project without mentioning the sounds Ana recorded, sounds that indicate a high probability of finding opal suits. Those distinguished gentlemen would have written us off as crazy. What I find crazy, though, is what their lack of curiosity and their obsequiousness have done to science.

Whoa, I sound just like my sister.

from: Dacia Arturo
to: Lucía Cocom Arturo
date: October 27, 2007 22:59
subject: Re: CAREFUL
They accepted the descent! Ana secured approval to enter the third level of the mine. A couple of medical researchers will come along to establish comparative parameters between the prototypes and the suits currently in use. The data's on our side, but wish us luck. We're going first thing on Saturday.

from: Lucia Cocom Arturo
to: Dacia Arturo
date: October 28, 2007 09:43
subject: BE VERY CAREFUL
Niña: I'm so glad. I hope everything goes well and you get the recognition you deserve. Don't even think of pushing it away. But I also want to tell you what's going on here so you can see what's coming. We're going to have to put up a fight. Be careful.

FORMER OFFICIALS, ENTREPRENEURS, AND REAL ESTATE DEVELOPERS DRIVE INDIGENOUS COMMUNITIES OFF THEIR LAND
Communal landowners and ejidatarios who possess sites attractive to property developers are pressured to leave, persuaded through legal ploys that reveal the collusion between agricultural officials and entrepreneurs to seize shared land; such figures are familiar with weak points in the law that may be exploited toward dissolving the protection of forests or communal property that would be otherwise illegal to sell. This network of corruption includes former governors, storied families of the Peninsula, and even pro-environmental NGOs, bankers, owners of ex-haciendas, and hoteliers.

October 28, 2007
I was about to respond to my sister with the news that Isidro has apparently gone missing. But I didn't feel like giving her reasons to feel vindicated when all I really want is a little comfort. Things are awful everywhere, as we know. Protesters live in peril until they're no longer alive, and no one ever does anything about it, period. It's hell. I hope Isidro is all right.
I've been thinking a lot about my fights with my sister in the time after the opal suits. I guess my current research—which felt like a new phase for me, although it's sent me back to that moment in every sense—is also evoking their lights and shadows. For example, the memory of when we'd drifted apart and she was so angry she could barely talk to me. The time we got into a screaming fight—when I told her I'd agreed to work for Diamondcorp—is seared into my mind.

"I can't believe this," she said. "It's like me telling you, 'Be right back, I'm going to spend the night with Comandante Téllez, the guy who had me disciplined for disobedience.'"

I defended myself: "What do you want me to do? We need money for the opal suits. And these people have the funds, it's not like they're giving me anything for free."

"Well it sounds to me like you've sold out on us," she retorted with a harsh laugh.

I was furious. "So what if I did? What's wrong with not wanting to beg for handouts from you and the government anymore?" I'd had enough with her self-righteous, self-martyring tone.

"Don't be an idiot! What I'm saying is that you can do better than working at the service of those monsters. All you'll get to do is tell them where to stick their dicks in the dirt so they can fill it with filth and make their millions. Is that what you want?"

What I really wanted, I thought then, was to travel the world to find and rescue all the opal suits I could, to understand them and protect whatever it was they produced—but I was exhausted, sick and tired of all the bullshit, and she was making me feel guilty.

"I want to stop living hand to mouth," I told her. "At least I'm ambitious. At least I want to get out of the muck." I regretted it as soon as I spoke. She wasn't going to drop it this time. I could see her disappointment.

"Of course, that's why you stopped calling yourself a Cocom and now sign your name like a foreigner. Pretty smart, aren't you?"

I left, slamming the door behind me.

October 30, 2007

A truck would drive us down another long tunnel toward the entrance to the third level of the mine, just like the day I came to Naica. There were four of us on the team: Ana, Eusebi, Kepa—the two of them would stay by the entrance, watching our backs, monitoring Ana's and my state of health with the medical kit at the ready—and me. We'd compare the results obtained by the bracelets that monitor our vitals.

There were two men at the mouth of the tunnel. I thought they were plainclothes guards, since they had guns in their holsters. I stopped and rolled down the window to greet them and present the document authorizing our presence there, but before I could say a thing, one of them barked, "You can't go in."

The doors were open, even though we were the ones with the authority to open them.

"Here's the letter," Ana told him, holding out the signed, stamped paper. Glancing at the rearview mirror, I saw a third man approaching behind us, so I couldn't back out. He approached the passenger side, where Ana sat, then laughed and murmured something that sounded menacing.

"Tell them to send help," I yelled to Kepa and slammed on the accelerator. The truck lurched inside and we were soon subsumed in total darkness.

Unlike the other tunnel, this one didn't have the lights on all the time: another step we had to take. I switched on the headlamps, and although I didn't know exactly how many kilometers stretched out before us, I drove as fast as I could. I heard Kepa's voice describing the situation over the radio, the enervating acoustic effect of the air, coming in hotter and hotter through a half-open window, mixing with Eusebi's voice as he swore. I heard Ana saying something to me, too. And then, suddenly, the murmur. The steam of the mine was infernal. Our faces and clothes were already drenched with sweat.

"Don't stop, Dacia. Help is on the way," Kepa said.

A radiant dot appeared before us and swiftly split in two: it was another truck careening toward us.

"Get down!" Ana shouted. I flung myself onto the wheel and felt the vehicle shooting past, almost close enough to graze us. Probably associates of the men who'd tried to keep us from coming in. The downward slope got steeper and I felt like I wouldn't be able to brake.

"Do you hear that?" I said.

"What's that noise?" Eusebi asked.

And Ana: "That's what we're here to find out."

The headlamps of the truck finally shone onto the entrance to the mine. It seemed to be locked. Those men clearly had a set of keys.

"Could there be someone inside?" Kepa asked.

"I don't think so. That truck would have stopped us," Eusebi said.

I parked and we got out, ignoring Eusebi, who protested that we should wait for instructions, we should cancel everything, it was dangerous to go down. I walked right to the switchboard.

"The keys, Ana," I said, and she tossed them to me. I flicked the switches and everything around us lit up. I opened the gate with nervous fingers, then the door to the entrance. Ana got the equipment ready as I opened door after door. The flickering signal of Kepa and Eusebi's radios ricocheted off the tunnel walls. Ana and I peeled off our sweat-soaked layers and pulled on the suits over our underwear, covering our boots. I noticed some *Aglossa pinguinalis*, mothlike cave butterflies, fluttering incessantly around us.

We stepped into the mine. The erratic beams illuminated our hands as we adjusted the harnesses, adjusting the ropes. Eusebi and Kepa kept the lab on the line and we all followed the protocol, distracted as we were. We made sure the suits were properly in place, our bracelets working, our watches in sync. I was grateful that the medics didn't put up more of a fight. They seemed impressed that Ana and I were so eager to find out what was happening.

We began our descent: the rock shuddered. The murmurs intensified; the source of the sound was close. Ana and I knew we couldn't dawdle even for a minute; impossible to know when we'd get another chance like this one. Centuries, maybe. We moved quickly down the shaft, which was pretty wide, maybe twenty meters across.

The headlamps on our helmets cast a dim light. When our feet touched the ground, we felt the vibrations like blows to the belly, to the soles of our feet. Ana unbuckled the recorder case from her belt and got it ready. Holding the microphone and moving around in her suit, which glowed phosphorescent in the beam of my helmet, she looked like a creature from another planet or another time.

Abruptly, the vibration was so jarring that I felt like something was wrong with my eardrums. I felt the murmur thrumming through my body. My sternum vibrated. The vitreous body of my sclera vibrated.

Up ahead and to the right, along the path of the old mine, we could see a whitish glow, like a light source reflected in water. My vision blurred and my eyes ached. I remembered hearing about people whose retinas had detached from the force of certain vibrations. I was scared, but I wanted to keep going, to make our way forward. I trusted the protective suit. The murmur was a chant, a battering, as if thousands of people were stamping on the rock. It was a song, in a way: a voice called out as the echoing thousands hammered their response into the stone.

What the hell was that? My pulsometer sounded an alarm. Ana asked in a gesture if I was all right, and I gave her a thumbs-up; she did the same. I was a bit unsettled by all the butterflies in the air. Why were they swarming us this way?

Then I caught the scent. It was certainly powerful, but we hadn't noticed it until then; our gas masks must have filtered out most of it. We stopped and slowly cast our light around us. To the left, our headlamps showed a pile of things I couldn't make out. I thought I caught a glimpse of embroidery that looked like a shirt of Isidro's we'd oohed and aahed over a few weeks back. Ana grabbed my arm, hard.

The vibration returned, slamming us with an intensity that couldn't have been under 50 m/s², if I'd been able to read the accelerometer.

"The suits work," I thought. "If we weren't wearing them, the vibration could strip our tendons from our bones until they looked like that: naked. In this humidity and temperature, we'd turn to food for those butterflies that graze on decomposed fat. The suits work. My god, someone dropped them all the way down here," I thought as I started to grasp—at the same time as I rejoiced at the success of the Disasters—the horror before us.

I groped for Ana's hand, her shoulder. Along with a violent wave of nausea, I felt stupid and stubborn in my futile desire to chase after the earth's mysteries, my longing for redemptive discoveries when the world is falling apart, dominated by the monsters we are.

Yet the song murmured something else. I couldn't say what, but it was the mystery itself. The redemptive discovery. And it was comforting.

Affected by the force of the vibrations, Eusebi and Kepa couldn't come down until the shaking had eased. The rescue team summoned by their calls for help had lots of questions for us.

from: Ana Otálora
to: Dacia Arturo
date: November 9, 2007 21:09
subject: Forensic report
My dear Dacia,
I want you to know that I understand why you didn't want to spend another minute here. What's happening would have been unbearable for you. Besides the violence and impunity all around us, we've revived, in a way, the bullheadedness and belittlement you've already been through before.

In the face of how hard the company worked to cover everything up and act as if nothing had happened, I just didn't know what to do—until you showed up in a dream I had. We were in the woods. You were showing me a book on my parents' shelf, a story I liked to read when I was little: "The Sing-ing Bone." Then we listened together to the strange, beautiful music of the opal vibrations. I was trained to believe that a dream is nothing but a dream. But I was so amazed that I called my mom and asked her to read me the story again. The bone, turned into a flute, told the tale of its own tragedy through music: it was actually a boy who'd been killed by his brother. The music led the others to seek justice and put his soul to rest. That's when I knew what to do.

I contacted Isidro's family and suggested they request a bone densitometry as part of the official autopsy, and, if possible, that they recommend the same to the families of other missing people who might be down there. I wrote up a document ex-plaining why the procedure could help shed light on the circumstances of his death, although, frankly, I wasn't sure it would contribute much to the investi-gation itself. What I had in mind, though, was that if you were right, it could help his family find solace.

I want to assure you, Dacia, that your ideas about the opal suits have always been headed in the right direction. You can be confident of that. Isidro's bones, and surely the bones of the other people whose remains we found in the mine, underwent the same metamorphic process. His skeleton, so to speak, is a set of iridescent opal fossils, reflecting light with all the colors of the rainbow. On the inside, they show the telltale fractures that likely contain the sonic information of the vibration that produced them. That indescribable music. Do you remember what that murmur seemed to say? I haven't forgot-ten it. We have to keep researching, Dacia. Please don't give up. I hope you'll come back.

I'm attaching the forensic report on the bones of our dear Isidro, whose song will keep singing. We'll make sure of it.

[Handwritten note from Dacia Arturo to her sister Lucía Cocom. The seal of the sender's office is crossed out with permanent marker. Approximate date: December 2009]

Lucía, please give this notebook to the ASCSOS for me. Tell them it contains information that, while it wasn't produced as part of our research project, will help expand our knowledge of the opal suits. Wish me luck, because I won't be back anytime soon. Take care of yourself, Luc. Do whatever you have to do.

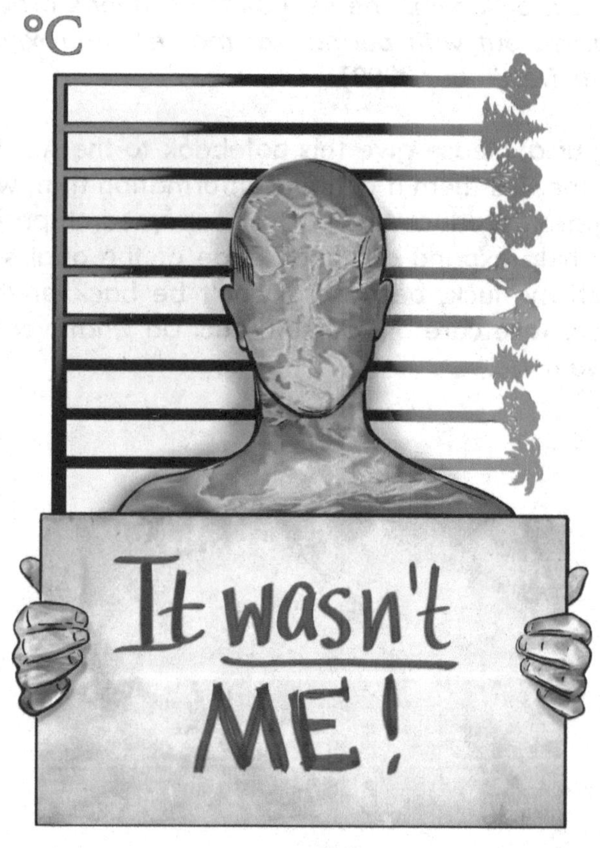

Illustration by Olga Pak

CARRY THAT WEIGHT

by Victor Fernando Ocampo

Victor Fernando R. Ocampo is the author of the International Rubery Book Award shortlisted *The Infinite Library and Other Stories* (Math Paper Press, 2017 ; US edition: Gaudy Boy, 2021) and *Here be Dragons* (Canvas Press, 2015), which won the Romeo Forbes Children's Story Award in 2012. His play-by-email interactive fiction piece *The Book of Red Shadows* debuted at the Singapore Writers Festival in 2020. His writing has appeared in many publications including Apex Magazine, Daily Science Fiction, Likhaan Journal, Strange Horizons, Philippines Graphic, Science Fiction World and The Quarterly Literature Review of Singapore, as well as anthologies like The Best New Singapore Short Stories, Fish Eats Lion: New Singaporean Speculative Fiction, LONTAR: The Journal of Southeast Asian Speculative Fiction, the Philippine Speculative Fiction series and Mapping New Stars: A Sourcebook on Philippine Speculative Fiction. He is a fellow at the Milford Science Fiction Writers' Conference (UK) and the Cinemalaya Ricky Lee Film Scriptwriting Workshop, as well as a Jalan Besar writer-in-residence at Sing Lit Station (2020/2021). Visit his blog at vrocampo.com or follow him on Twitter @VictorOcampo

At the crack of dawn, the two brothers left their habitat. Carrying their waterproof phones and open-mesh baskets made from recycled plastic, they walked almost barefoot on the non-slip edge of the platform's enormous starfish arms, towards where the Sargassum beds lay.

The blue-green sea was calm that morning, still weighed down by the wind.

The young men walked rapidly, the older one was two or three steps ahead, while the younger, more awkward boy, was trailing in his wake.

The sun advanced just as quickly as the two had walked, banishing the shadows away from everything save for the dark mountains in the heart of the distant Quezon mainland. Contact lenses automatically formed over the boys' eyes, reducing the glare and blocking the sun's harmful UVA/UVB rays.

Eventually, the two brothers reached the boat pier at the end of the platform. The older brother stopped to check his phone.

"Is the satellite overhead, Kuya Berto?" the younger boy asked.

"It's always overhead," the older one answered, as he activated his garbage-collecting basket and threw it into the water. As soon as it landed, the bulbous, sea-squirt-shaped device began hunting and sucking up microplastics. "Better get yours ready, Lucas, or you won't get paid."

The younger boy carefully placed his basket on the water and switched it on. It made a sad, wheezing sound before powering down.

"Do you ever clean the filter?" Berto asked. "It looks like we'll need to replace it."

"I had so much homework last night. I forgot."

"Right. I'll let it go this time—again—but you really need to be more responsible," Berto said.

"Every carbon coin we make can help Papa get better. They've just cleared quarantine. His surgery's tomorrow."

"I know. I'm sorry."

"Just watch my basket," Berto said, as he took of his wind breaker and shucked off his shorts. "I'm going to check the Sargassum beds."

The smaller boy watched as his brother fished out a pair of smart goggles from his shorts pocket and clipped his phone to his wristband. Berto's body was dark and tightly muscled. He seemed naked save for the skintight nanotech body suit that kept his body warm and protected it from the sun's radiation.

"You're not using a rebreather?" Lucas asked.

"I'm practicing for the free diving competition in May," Berto said. "The prize is one full carbon coin."

"I won't tell Mama and Papa, if you won't tell them about my basket filter."

"Deal."

Berto dove into the dark waters. A special sensor on his phone immediately ran diagnostics on the water quality around him and on the health of the sargassum forest that hung vertically from the bottom of their platform. The information he collected was sent to a satellite overhead, where a SEA-DAO contract paid them carbon tokens if their produce improved the water quality in their section of Tayabas Bay.

The young man went down past five meters, then eight meters before pushing himself even deeper until he reached the very edge of the seaweed blades at almost 12 meters deep.

At the heart of the ocean, Berto felt free. In the darkness of the depths, he could let go of everything—his father's illness, his mother's depression, their never-ending money problems, the tax pirates that constantly threatened their savings, and poor, lost Julia. He especially did not want to think about her. Instead, he concentrated on overcoming his urge to breathe until he became completely aware of his body and the infinity of where he was, until he was entirely lost in the moment.

Meanwhile, at the far edge of the pier, Lucas was starting to get worried. Eight full minutes had gone by since his kuya had disappeared under the water.

Suddenly, Berto broke for air near the boat slip at the middle of the floating dock. He clung loosely to the swimming ladder for several moments and then vaulted up, vigorously shaking off the seawater that rolled off his nanotech suit. The material was so thin that Lucas could clearly see the tattoo of the Bakunawa dragon hidden on his brother's back.

Berto straightened abruptly and in the moment he seemed to stand on the horizon, his head touching the endless sky. Judging by the way his brother swaggered back, Lucas knew that everything was alright.

"Your basket's full," Lucas reported. "That means more money!"

The boy beamed, he knew that once they returned to their habitat, another smart contract would interact with the basket, auctioning the microplastic for more carbon tokens.

Berto smiled weakly. Despite the SEA-DAO contracts that he set up, he knew that they were still quite a long way off from earning the credits their parents needed.

"Every little bit helps," he said, as he slipped his shorts back on and zipped up his windbreaker. He folded his goggles back into his pocket.

Lucas was happy, and when that happened, he became quite chatty. He searched his mind for something interesting to say to his brother. Then he remembered the *bagis*, a rare megamouth shark with a huge bounty on its head. Berto's hidden tattoo had reminded him of it.

"Did you see anything strange down there?" he asked excitedly. "Any large sharks with big glowing mouths?"

The younger boy knew everything about the strange, planktivorous creature with an extremely large mouth on its fat, bulbous head. He and his friends talked about it interminably during free periods at their Metaverse school. Lucas knew all about its habits, its mystery, and most of all, he knew about how it had eluded scientists for years. The reward for the decades-old IoT sensor data that the bagis carried would be enough to pay for their father's treatments and sustain their family for a year.

"Will you stop it about the bagis?" Berto said. "Look, a few people thought they saw it once, years ago, and no one's seen it ever again. Honestly? I think it's a myth. There was never any ping back from its IoT black box."

"But two people died because of it."

"A megamouth shark eats plankton," Berto said, now mildly irritated. "I heard that story too. Supposedly, those idiots were tax pirates. They killed each other trying to get the sensor bounty. That data on ocean currents would be pretty valuable."

Lucas was about to say something but he spied a small dark shape looming on the horizon.

"Kuya, look!" he shouted.

The proximity klaxon on their phones roared to life.

"Pirates!" Berto said. "Get back to the habitat, now! Get ready to submerge."

"But what about you?"

"I need to stay and engage them."

"Why?"

"Do as I say!" the older brother commanded. "Go!"

Startled into action, the younger boy ran back to their quarters like some fleeing, flightless bird.

A small motorized paraw appeared in the distance and advanced towards the boat slip. As the double outrigger sail boat came nearer, Berto spied a familiar scruffy figure sitting on the banka. He was smoking and drinking something from a small metal cup. Berto stared at the young man's cigarette as it unwound its skein of blue-grey smoke into the unpolluted air.

"Hoy, Berto!" the man shouted.

"What do you want, Isko?"

Berto's nanotech suit automatically formed a mask that covered half his face.

"Is that any way to treat a dear friend?" he said as he moored the paraw against the pier.

Isko seemed to be the same age as Berto but taller and brawnier. He jumped onto the platform and walked towards the brooding young man.

Berto fixed his stare upon at the newcomer. Isko smiled and took another drag from his cigarette.

"It's that time of the month again."

"We don't have enough credits. My father just had another operation in the mainland."

"Is that so?" Isko said. "Indonesia's Hainuwele Clan has been encroaching more and more into our territory. Have you checked your farm for ransomware lately?"

Berto said nothing.

"The Ching Shih have also been detected here in Quezon. The *Ching Shih*," Isko repeated. "You know, the ones your sister Julia hacked with that spectacular Shamoon-style exploit? I'm sure they'll be out for blood if they find you guys. We can protect you and your family, you know. But you need to keep up your subscription fee. Your Papa always paid it but someone cancelled the SEA-DAO contract last week."

"Don't say her name," Berto growled.

"Careful, Berto," Isko growled back. "Julia was a proud and valued member of the Pintados. She wore the Bakunawa with pride. Don't forget how your family got the coin for this vertical farm in the first place, and she's why mother's so lenient with you."

"The Pintados got Julia killed," Berto retorted. "She came back to us in pieces. Mama's never been the same since."

Isko sighed and took Berto's hand. "Let's start over again, shall we?" he said softly. "Sit with me, please."

The two men squatted on the floating pier.

"Why did you cancel our SEA-DAO contract?" Isko asked. "Luckily, I intercepted the report before the AI auditors got to it."

"Thank you."

"Apart from breaking the contract, that's a week without the Pintado's threat intelligence data."

"I put perimeter buoys. I was going to renew."

"The Ching Shih could have already found you."

"Papa's dying," Berto said. "I needed to funnel all our tokens for his transplant. The Philippine government's barely functional. We needed to pay so many bribes just to get him a surgery slot. I really had no choice."

"You could come back to the Pintados," Isko asked. "I always thought you were a better tax pirate than your older sister. Mother will still probably let you trade code on the Haradhere Exchange in Somalia, if you want to."

"I'm the eldest now, my family needs me," Berto said. "Someone has to manage this farm, especially when the off-season typhoons hit."

"My booster's updated. I want to see your face."

Berto swiped away his nanotech mask.

"I'm sorry but you still need to pay the back taxes," Isko insisted. "Do you have any alternatives?"

"Lucas and I salvaged a large tank during the last super-typhoon," Berto said. "We've converted it into an anaerobic digestion chamber to make biogas from the sargassum. I think we made enough fuel to pay for this month, if you don't mind accepting in-kind payment. If that's not enough, we also collected a lot of industrial salvage from the trash gyre off Pagbilao Grande."

"The biofuel will do. I'll send over a robo-paraw with a tanker to collect tomorrow," Isko answered. "You'll need to write up a new SEA-DAO contract with an in-kind clause. Your folks are exposed in Manila. Better check up on them."

"I will," Berto said softly. "Thanks."

"Are you sure I can't get you to come back to us?" Isko asked.

When Berto didn't answer, Isko lit another cigarette and returned to his paraw.

Berto watched as his friend's boat disappeared into the distance. He heard an old song from the Beatles' *Abbey Road* play on Isko's torrent stream and fade into the wind.

When the paraw was gone, Berto stripped back down to his nanotech suit and returned to the water. This time he stayed under for a full eleven minutes.

Along the dock pilings, a hidden security drone took advantage of Berto's absence. It stopped recording and swiftly flew towards the family habitat.

When Berto returned to his quarters, he found Lucas waiting impatiently, arms crossed and his face crumpled with a mix of worry and anger.

"Who was that guy?" the younger brother asked. "Why were you so friendly with a Pintado?"

"He's an old classmate," Berto said defensively, "We interned together after open university."

"I'm 15, not an idiot," Lucas retorted. The younger boy sent a drone cam still from his phone to all the media tiles in the room. It was a close-up of a Bakunawa tattoo on the strangers back. "He's a Pintado. So are you."

"Not anymore. It's complicated," Berto answered. "Why were you spying on me?"

"Really?" Lucas cried out. "I got worried when I couldn't access the outside camera feeds. You locked me out of the system. I tried to use Julia's cracker to brute force your password but your encryption's too good."

"So you sent a security drone to spy on your kuya?" Berto said, his voice rising. "You need to stay out of this. I'm trying to keep you safe."

"You lied to me. Do Papa and Mama know?"

"Yes."

"You all lied to me!" Lucas yelled. "Ate Julia was murdered because of the Pintados!"

"Ate Julia was their best hacker," Berto said softly. "The Pintados didn't kill her."

"What?"

"She was murdered by the Red Flag Ching Shih from the floating city of Kwongchow," Berto explained. "Her biggest hack brought down their Red Flag DAO and transferred a third of their tokens to the Taiwan Autonomous Zone."

"I read about that in code school," Lucas said. "But I don't believe you. That was an anonymous attack. I don't remember reading anything about Pintados being involved. Well, there was some chatter on the pirate boards."

"Julia was that anonymous hacker," Berto said. "That's how we got this farm. It's also why she was murdered on her way to Somalia. I was supposed to be on the same airship but I got into a fight with the son of the Pintado's Lakambini. I should have been with her. I could have protected her."

"But you didn't."

"I don't want to talk about it... not right now," Berto said. "All I know is that I don't want to lose any of you again."

"I can take care of myself."

"Probably."

"No more lies, kuya." Lucas insisted. "No more secrets. Did the Ching Shih go after the Pintados?"

"No, Ate Julia made it look like a lone wolf attack. They had murdered Kuan-lin the year before. Remember him, her fiancée?"

"I do. But that doesn't mean they won't come after us too."

"I'm sure they will. Eventually," Berto said. "But, I'll deal with it. I'm the eldest now. Papa's too sick and Mama needs to take care of him."

"No," Lucas insisted, "You need to keep me in the loop. I need to share the burden too or we all die."

"I guess you're almost as old as I was when I joined the Pintados. I suppose I should have told you."

"*I suppose?*" Lucas asked. "No more secrets!"

"No more secrets."

"Show me your tattoo."

Berto unzipped his windbreaker and turned off the skintight nanotech suit that covered his muscular upper body. He turned his back to show the serpent-like dragon with a looped tail and a horn on its nose that was tattooed like a black ink painting on his dark skin.

"When were you recruited?"

"Ate Julia brought me in during my sophomore year of uni. I helped create the modular virus she used to take down their DAO."

Lucas traced the tattoo on his brother's back. "Large mouth, fat, bulbous head," The boy mumbled. "I wonder if pre-historic megamouth sightings became the Bakunawa myth?"

"What? No. Megamouths were only discovered in the twentieth century," Berto said. "What the hell does the bagis have to do with our situation?"

"*Discovered* is such an awful, colonizer word," Lucas mused. "In any case, we need credits for Papa, right? You'll use up all our biogas to pay the Pintados. That's our immediate issue. The sooner they get back home the sooner we can harden the farm against the Chinese pirates."

"Oh God, you're in one of your obsessive phases," Berto said. "I really can't deal with this right now."

"Just trust me, please."

Berto said nothing. He got up and made himself a cup of sargassum tea.

"Please?"

After a few more minutes of silence Berto finally spoke. "Sigh. What do you want to do?"

Lucas pulled up the code he was working on and sent it to the largest screen in their habitat.

"I found a database from the Woods Hole Oceanographic Institution with data on every known megamouth sighting since 1976. I cross-referenced that with the nearest deep water area where there's a known Bakunawa legend. Then I wrote a predictive algo to plot where it may appear next. The bagis has a wide range but it travels very slowly, only about 2 km per day. According to my calculations we are due for another sighting right here in Tayabas Bay. I've been making small adjustments to the farm's drift to steer us on an intercept course."

"Go on."

"So I repurposed a couple of your perimeter buoys to ping the frequency of its telemetry black box and... listen!"

All the media tiles in the habitat rang with the same loud "ping".

"Fuck!" The older boy spat out his tea.

Berto fired up his system and began hacking into megamouth's tracker.

"The bagis' IoT device is ancient." The older brother said, "It still uses insecure and flawed design protocols. Give me a few minutes."

Lucas got a rag to clean up his brother mess. "Are you in?" he asked.

"Bingo!"

The two brothers cheered as they downloaded decades-old data on ocean currents, water quality, and climate information.

"Do you want to do the honors?" Berto asked.

"Yes, Kuya," Lucas squealed with delight as he sent the data to an American Smart Contract satellite. After a few minutes of verification, it sent the full reward credits to their family's crypto wallet.

Berto hugged his little brother tightly. "I think we can pay off the Pintados, renew our protection contract, and still have more than enough credits to pay Papa's medical bill."

"We should call Mama and Papa," Lucas added.

Berto ordered his terminal to contact their mother's phone.

"The party you are calling is not available."

The brothers tried calling six times but their parents remained unreachable.

Berto messaged his mother over the Pintado's secure satellite link. There was no response.

"Keep trying," Lucas said.

"Maybe there's no connectivity in the ICU. I'll let the system keep trying."

"Can you ping their phones?"

"No."

Berto closed his eyes and wrapped his arms over his head.

"What are you doing?" Lucas asked.

"I'm calling a friend for help."

Berto let out a deep sigh and asked his terminal to connect him to Isko.

"What do you want, Berto?" Isko's scowling face appeared on all the media tiles.

"I need your help."

"You have a lot of nerve. I already helped you out today."

"Please," Berto pleaded. "I just need the Pintados to check if my parents are safe in QC."

"Why should I help you? You didn't want to help us."

"Isko, please."

After a long pause, Isko sighed and said. "Fine, but you owe me. Again. Where are they, exactly?"

"They're at the ICU of St. Luke's Hospital in Quezon City."

"Okay," Isko said. "Let me make a couple of calls and get back to you."

The son of the Pintado's Lakambini hung up. Less than five minutes later he called back.

"Berto," Isko warned. "You need to get out of there! Something's happened."

He sent a couple of news reports on the media tiles. Most of them ran the same horrific story.

Breaking News: 14 killed, 75 wounded in bomb attack

at the St. Luke's Hospital in Quezon City.

Philippine military officials say a drone attack of unknown origin hit the top three floors of the St. Luke's Hospital in Quezon City that together killed 14 people, many of them at the Intensive Care Unit of the 650-bed hospital. The bombing was staged as the government grapples with the highest number of mutant coronavirus infections in Southeast Asia, as well as the growing number of militant breakaway Autonomous Pirate Zones around the region.

"You need to get out of there Berto!" Isko repeated. "Without our threat data your system's probably compromised. The Ching Shih killed your folks. They'll come after you next. Please leave, now!"

Before either brother could react, the children's song *Baby Shark* suddenly started playing across the entire habitat.

"Fuck!" Berto screamed. "What the fuck is that?"

"I rigged the system to alert us once the megamouth crosses our perimeter," Lucas said, as he shut down the jury-rigged alarm. "I'm sorry."

The younger brother began to cry. "Mama," Lucas whimpered. "Papa."

"I can send a paraw to get you both," Isko said. "Pack up your stuff. I'm sorry about your folks. I really am, but you can mourn later."

As Berto and Isko were talking, *Baby Shark* started blasting from the speakers once again.

"Fuck!" Berto shouted angrily. "SHUT THAT OFF!"

Lucas stopped crying. "That means there's a second shark coming our...."

Berto pulled up the farm's storm LIDAR. The proximity klaxons on their phones also started to blare urgently.

"That's not a shark," he yelled.

He grabbed his younger brother and quickly shoved him into an emergency pod just before a large explosion tore through their habitat. A second, larger explosion destroyed their biogas facility.

"Berto!" Lucas screamed as the escape pod rocketed underwater towards a pre-programmed route to Pagbilao Grande.

The water rushed into the mangled habitat, along with a wall of hard metal rain. Berto was swept beneath the cold sea, through deadly currents swirling with torn seaweed and aquaculture debris. The young man's body became numb. But just before the moment when he completely lost muscle control, he felt a violent kick strike him on the face.

He rolled underwater and crashed into an oyster-filled support piling. The shells sliced through his windbreaker, but his nigh-indestructible nanotech suit kept his skin from being torn to pieces.

When his reflexes returned, he sucked in his belly and the taut webs of air in his body slackened. Eventually, the sea buoyed him up to the surface.

A sharp pain pierced his ears. Berto felt like his skull was bursting, but fear and adrenaline kept his mind clear.

For a moment Berto wondered if it would be easier to just sink back to the depths and never resurface. Everything he and his family had built—had died for—was lost.

Then he remembered Lucas.

The young man turned over and began to swim towards the habitat's wreckage.

He spied an intact server unit floating in the water. Berto felt for his phone in his pocket and started salvaging all the data he could. With comms gone, he could neither upload to the cloud nor call for help.

The sun had already set and the sea was turning inky black.

Suddenly a bone-white beam of light swept across the water's surface. Berto was about to wave for help when he realized that he didn't recognize the boat's make or model. Two burly men emerged from the galleys and started burning the floating debris with a flamethrower.

The young man knew he had only one option to survive. He took an enormous gulp of air and dived down as deep as his injured body would take him. Six meters, eight meters, he kept swimming until he returned to the dark heart of the sea, nursing his grief and anger like talismans.

At the crack of dawn, Lucas finally located his brother's phone. Isko and his men had to cut through Berto's nanotech suit which had formed an emergency re-breather cocoon around his body.

Later that morning, Berto sat at the prow of Isko's paraw, staring at the ominous gray squall forming near the mainland.

"I'm coming back," he whispered as he sipped sargassum tea from a metal cup. "I managed to salvage this."

Berto produced a small bottle with a germling of Sargassum aquifolium from their vertical farm.

"Oh, and Ate Julia's modular virus," he added grimly. "Lucas and I are going to fucking wipe the Red Flag Ching Shih from cyberspace."

He reached out for Isko's hand. "Sit with me?" Both men stared into the distance. The blue-green sea was calm that morning, still weighed down by the wind.

Illustration by Daniela Zucca

CARRANCA

by Aline Valek

translated by G.Holleran

Aline Valek is a Brazilian writer and illustrator, living in Munich, Germany. Born in Minas Gerais, also the birthplace of renowned author João Guimarães Rosa, and raised in the airplane-shaped "utopian" city of Brasília, Aline has written and self-published since her teenage years. Since the beginning of her career, Aline made the internet her creative territory. Her work is multiplatform: she creates across a variety of spaces, including her blog, newsletter, fanzines, podcasts and books. Aline has several short-stories published in anthologies and magazines. She has self-published her own collections of short-stories, including her most recent work, *Neuroses a Varejo* (Retail Neuroses), a collection that explores the lives of four women dealing with absurd disorders. Author of the oceanic sci-fi novel *As Águas-vivas Não Sabem De Si* (Jellyfish Lack Self Awareness) and the apocalyptic portrait of Brazil in the novel *Cidades afundam em dias normais* (Cities Sink on Normal Days), Aline introduces her readers to new worlds through the lens of intriguing, intelligent, complex female protagonists. Aline also tells stories about the hidden wonders of history, science, art and language in her podcast *Bobagens Imperdíveis* (Shenanigans You Can't Miss). More about her work can be found on her online planet: alinevalek.com.br

It's best to avoid effort. Why trouble your head over something you can't resolve? It isn't worth it. In Pitiguyri we wait for things to happen in their own time, knowing the resolution will unfold while we chat, while we watch kids play their video games, while we scroll through the pages of a book, while the rain pours and there isn't much to do besides watch the ground suck up the water. Dwelling on calculation and occupying the mind with problems is why we have machines—let them take care of it.

Clever is the one that likes to get together and hear stories. Smoke a cigarette and watch the time burn. The ideas line up on their own in the listening, like dreams falling slowly into place, no need to force it. Even so, it takes a while.

I met a headstrong guy once, whose thoughts were also clouded with problems. He came by here some time ago, but not to visit Pitiguyri like you are. It was a short trip. He possessed the poverty of being unable to wait.

At that time, the community was much smaller. It didn't even have the underground floors, down where it's cooler and the machines can think without having to expend so much energy. Everybody likes the fresh air, even in this heat that seems to want our bodies to stay horizontal. Cats have the right idea, stretched out in their hanging hammocks. And it was right around the Free Time Festivities, one of the few times a year when the people all mobilise at once, simply because they want to. You have to see it to understand that partying is taken seriously here. It is during the festivities that we celebrate our conquest over this lifestyle in which being busy is completely optional, so it's a pleasure to be busy with the preparations. Music and dance rehearsals, work-shops in full swing with people designing costumes while machines stitch fabrics, the back-and-forth of a robot carrying decorations, people engrossed in programming light shows, planning menus full of rare flavours, painting murals with bioluminescent bacteria, creating giant wind-powered automata to parade like snakes, preparing video games that rec-reate long-extinct environments or tell stories told never before. All of this would be presented during the Festivities, which over the centuries have be-come a time and place to showcase talents, ideas. Everything that makes us human. This cauldron of bubbling words.

That year I was involved in imagination produc-tion. The world has come a long way since the first myths were conceived. Today they are worn out, bits and pieces of beliefs. Our dreaming lacked an origin myth that was more in tune with our life, without all those punishments and authorities and prohibitions. Gods who punished disobedient children with work, or asked heroes to take on missions. Weariness, suf-fering! It would no longer do. None of the Genesis that were passed down included rest and machines. They, who freed human flesh from the scourge of labour, were the reason the Festivities existed! How could they not also be in the songs and paintings and obscure metaphors embedded into a video game to make us sigh and suddenly understand everything?

A great responsibility, but it wasn't hard work. On the contrary, overexertion only gets in the way of this writing. My job was to go to the workshop in the morning, step into a voice loop, and recall the images and symbols that had revealed themselves to me in my dreams, just the same as I'd tell you about something I saw happen long ago.

The loop logged word after word and displayed them in writing, scrolling across the screen. The more relevant to the story or charged with emotion, the bigger the words got. Other storytellers' words were shuffling in the machine's memory, words left there on other mornings over the course of months. When I finished my recollection, I liked to go back and listen, in the smooth voice made of codes, to the story being spun from that tangled knot of merged meanings. Everything seemed to indicate that the myth to be presented at the Festivities would speak of tunnels at the beginning of everything. Serpents streaking across the sky, the formation of rivers, or the cables connecting the first machines. Umbilical cords, if you think about it, or the spiralling strands of our DNA, are essentially the same idea. The stories told varied day by day as new dreams were inputted into the loop, but the pattern that was forming was tubular, traverse. From some chaotic place to our paradise.

I went outside to roll a cigarette, feeling new ideas arriving, ideas about how to stitch together a story with what I had just heard. I found a patch of shade to sit in and watched some brothers tuning up their instruments in the town square, the strings and percussion still out of sync.

All around, a buzzbuzz that wasn't coming from the music, nor from conversation, nor from the general milling about that the Festivities inspired, but a nagging, unwelcome noise that comes right before a sting on the skin. Mosquitoes!

I slapped my hand on my neck, grimacing. I was already starting to feel that burning itch in places difficult to scratch, right around the ankle bone, you know the feeling?

It was still common to feel one or two on the hottest days, landing on the patterned veins of distracted folks. No, nothing out of the ordinary, considering that beyond the radius of our community, mosquitoes abound in clouds. That's where the danger lies.

I've heard the stories ever since I was a little kid. A large, grown man who'd trampled through desert swamplands, skin exposed, unprotected. Drained to the last drop, covered in a crust of giant mosquitoes. Imagine seeing something like that... No one is crazy enough to put legends to the test when they already know the pain of a mosquito-scorpion's sting. Just imagine being captured by a cloud of them.

I asked a sister if she'd felt an excessive presence of mosquitoes that morning.

"It seems like it," she replied.

We realised in astonishment that the bites had been happening more frequently for several days now. Could it be a defect in a carranca? We immediately began to speculate.

At that time, there were many carrancas surrounding the perimeter of Pitiguyri, a box around this big, programmed to drive away various pests, the creepy-crawlies, the parasites, the ones that bite and sting. It could measure the environment and adjust the size of the waves accordingly to repel unwanted fauna.[1]

____

1 In Brazilian culture, a *carranca* (which literally translates to 'scowl') designates a specific kind of figurehead that was intended to protect ships from the river's unkind spirits, a concept derived from indigenous culture. Carrancas were used principally on the Rio São Francisco in Northeast Brazil dating

"There must be a bug in the latest update. Don't worry, the system will fix it soon."

I had to be right. Everyone's mind was on the Festivities, they must have not seen the warning in the system about such a small error.

I went to the Machine Room to take care of whatever had happened. I dialled up a Beadle, which started to beam letters onto the screen.

"Good morning, my sister," she said, and I asked her to open the control panel. Lots of status checks on the crops, updates from the factories, indications of appliances in need of repair. Some of the machines had repaired themselves, but it looked like none of them were carrancas. All of them lit up green on the map.

I asked the Beadle to update the signal. There it was. One little dot turned red.

Could there be an open gateway where the shameless gnats were getting in?

The Beadle couldn't say what had happened to the carranca; it wasn't coming up for her anymore.

Dismayed, I went to find Ueder straightaway. My son, the bearded fellow you met the other day, then a young boy, apprenticed in the greenhouses. Just the right age to be willing to try all kinds of things. He was wearing headphones and spinning a turntable with his fingers, so he didn't hear me calling, immersed as he was in extracting noises from a colony of mushrooms. I always found mushrooms to be too grating, lacking the melodious wisdom of cacti or the complex sound of palm trees.

---

back to the late eighteenth/early nineteenth centuries. They were traditionally carved from wood and painted, usually depicting humans or animals.

If these youngsters thought they could get music from that, so be it. Mum isn't judging. I told him about the carranca without a signal, about the idea that occurred to me to spy from a distance to find a clue as to what had disconnected it.

"Why? Just get the Beadle to reset it."

I did that already. I know the face he makes when he wants to put off helping me, but this time I insisted that he cut it out and give me a hand, those mushrooms weren't going anywhere.

Half annoyed, half curious, he sent a Tucumã, a palm-size robot, to fly to the point I indicated on the map. We watched a screen on the wall to observe the images that were coming in. They quickly made us dizzy.

Ueder was used to navigating at that speed, which soon led a crowd of children to gather around us. The Tucumã flew, circling the area until he found the lost carranca, half-buried in muddy sand. The kids cheered. Ueder caught an unusual detail in the image: 'Uh, Mum... It wasn't just deactivated. It was dismantled.'

That was strange. Even stranger was the urge that overtook me to want to get a closer look, to hunt for the reason this happened. The stories we tell follow the tracks of the paths we take in life, pushing us almost to the point of unravelling. To tell a good story, you've got to live. Which is another way of saying I don't shy away from gossip. And even with that trembling swarm of mosquitos, I knew I had still better go.

I asked Ueder to prepare Carapinhé to pick me up at my doorstep. I got myself ready, put on a long cape, safety mask, gloves. Carapinhé arrived, his body gleaming from the good care my son gave him. I poured some coffee into a bottle.

"Where are we off to, my brother?"

Carapinhé opened his passenger cabin excitedly, but I'd be the one inside this time, and I'd already warned him not to mess with me by going too fast.

Ueder drew the path on the map that he'd learned from flying the Tucumã. I got in. The kids on the street chased after me, shouting 'go auntie!' and 'show us, auntie!', as if I were going to present a video game, imagine that? Oh, if only. I promised nothing and told Carapinhé to take off.

It took about an hour for us to reach the sandy marshes, where I got out and found the dismantled carcass of the carranca. From that distance, Pitiguyri looked more like a giant lying on its back, wrapped in a fuzzy blanket of trees. A landscape of comfort. The hills dappled with towers and solar panels on the houses, the forest only starting to thin far outside the heart of the community. A beauty to behold from afar, don't you agree?

As I stood there, observing the distance between there and any point through which someone could enter, I started to feel uneasy. The carranca was missing its crystals. In order to pull the lid off, you'd have to be a person, or at least an animal with thumbs.

Mushy earth, hard to leave a trail, so I staggered forward, Carapinhé behind me, his motor giving off a muffled vroom-vroom.

"Are we going toward those rocks, my sister? The ground you saw is 2 kilometres west of here."

A machine full of hunches and me trying to see if I could find any sort of footprint. A blazing sun. Whoever had passed through was going to want to find shelter soon. Toward the rocks we went.

As the boulders begin to crop up, I see an apparition in a dark cloak on a rocky hillside across the way. Broad and masked, it crouched near the mouth of a cave, doing who knows what with its hands. It looked at me, startled, and disappeared into the stone. I quickened my pace and immediately shouted to let it know I had caught sight of it, for it not to run away.

He was the one in danger, I thought, not me, not with Carapinhé by my side, ready to retaliate any attack. That figure must have been in a terrible situation, looking for a piece of something in the middle of that vast nothingness.

"You need some help?" I yelled feebly, balancing myself as I climbed over the rocks. After a long silence I heard a "No, I'm good, you can go," and I was suspicious of the voice that came forward without showing its face. Had he been the one to dislodge the carranca? I asked. With no desire to respond, he paused before speaking, but he confessed: "Okay, fine, it was me, but I had to do it."

"So why didn't you just ask, man? Had you walked a little longer and gotten to Pitiguyri, you would have found anything you could need."

He stayed silent, but I kept on climbing, until I was level with the cave's opening. I lowered the visor on my mask and showed myself from a distance as he sat there, a knapsack full of stuff spread out around him. It looked like he'd set up camp, a lunchbox on the ground—I must have interrupted his meal because I could still see some farofa.

"Thanks for your concern, ma'am, but I wouldn't have had time to go down there."

He slowly took his mask off, mostly to show he was telling the truth. His face had the look of someone who had travelled a long way, weariness in his eyes. Said he really needed the parts, if he could just make up for my loss, if I could take something from him in return. He'd carried so little with him, only the one piece of luggage and a cyclotron, beat-up from his journey. Running on even less than the basics.

I shook my bottle and offered: "Join me for a spot of coffee, then?"

He didn't say no. I poured him a cup and asked his name; he answered Xandris. He came from the Islands, he told me, and I was amazed that someone so alone and at risk had travelled such a long distance.

When I was a young girl, I visited the Islands to spend some time apprenticing. I was struck by the size of everything. The height of the towers, the number of people, the richness of the studies, the fine-tuned systems, the top-of-the-line machines, the nonstop stream of news and innovation.

There will always be so much more future there, I thought to myself, because the more people think together, the faster time speeds by. I told him my positive impression of the place, multitudes of water surrounding everything. A view to impress. Xandris retorted that it was not all wonders. Obviously, otherwise he wouldn't have fled here.

"Sometimes too many people can be a problem."

I agreed, I liked living where everyone knew each other, although at that time Pitiguyri's population was already not negligible.

"I was tired of all those people, if you really want to know. I'm on a sabbatical to take a break from that lifestyle. To look for a different one on my own."

And there I was, out of place, wanting to have a chat with a stranger, and I apologised for ruining his isolation.

"It's not your fault," he said to me, "this is why I took your crystals."

The crystals weren't mine. But every one of his responses just made me more curious.

"What do you mean, 'this is why'?"

"To avoid making any contact. To find a way to become invisible, to expel attention from people or machines."

I was sure the fellow must be unwell. I didn't know nor could I imagine how to convert a carranca from an animal and insect repellent to one that repels people, but the folks on the Islands had a reputation for ingenuity. The pilgrim had MacGyvered an addition to his mask and took some crystals out of it, flashing them between his dirty fingernails, laughing in an attempt to show kindness: "I'll have to make some adjustments, apparently, since you weren't repelled from me."

Of course it didn't work, but who was I to discourage the kid? Better yet, maybe it would protect him from the creatures in that crossing.

I told him that I didn't understand how people could be so bad when sometimes they show up to share coffee and conversation. To which he replied, unaware of my astonishment: "Leaving your city to come to this spot in the middle of nowhere to see a disconnected carranca with your own eyes? Anyone who makes a commitment like that must at least have some desire to be alone."

I'll be damned. I hadn't looked at it that way, but he must have fished some kind of truth out of me. The fact was, Pitiguyri was noisy, everyone involved in their own projects, and the excessive mosquitoes aside, I was looking for a space to think – silence, as it were. Distance. It seemed we had something in common, then. As if to apologise for crossing a line, Xandris explained that he had not had good experiences dealing with people and that he was practising solitude, a hermit by sport and by choice.

I kept quiet, open to hearing more. At times like these, all you need to do is sit and listen to the fable unfold. And the story was that he came from the Islands, he and his cyclotron, with no artificial intelligence to assist him on the way, heading for the central Brazilian desert, where he'd make a home with his own hands, to dwell indefinitely in total solitude.

I could understand the point of making such a journey, to pass through the far-off country, to contemplate nature in its raw state, which can also be quite untamed. But to do it all alone? Grow your own food, dig out your own water, construct your own shelter, repair your vehicle, somehow find the energy? Even thinking about it exhausted me. Too much work.

"Our ancestors lived like this for most of history. Harvesting, interpreting the environment, transforming things with their own hands, or with a stump of wood they picked up, using their own brain cells to come up with solutions. The human being is a survival machine."

I couldn't agree with that. The best part of existing can't come until after our survival is guaranteed! Our ancestors had also invented slavery, borders, plastic. They made talk shows, newspapers, sausages, among other nonsense. They had to look at their watches for everything. Ancestral doesn't mean good. Those who are alive today have the freedom to choose differently than people who died long ago. I argued. Back then, people had to worry about paying just to live on the planet! What other creature has done that? True, it would be great if the mosquitoes paid taxes. I put forward my doubts about willingly making things more difficult. To single-handedly concentrate so much worry into a fragile body of flesh. And what about free time? That didn't matter to Xandris. That guy was the opposite of his life in the Islands, unsustained by systems, without the company of a crowd, just him and his thoughts, and that came at a cost. After crossing part of the ocean, he ran into some people, shared some time with them, until he realised he really needed to go on alone.

He told me about passing through Porto Jacaré with its famous nightlife. The most beautiful place he'd ever set foot in, its squares resplendent with fruit trees, the spicy smells coming from the fish stalls, the charming Grutian-style architecture, everything round and bright, like beetles gathered in an orgy. When the sun set, its energy continued shining in the streetlights, in the panels in the town squares, in the glow from the arcades, in the people's laughter, in the skin paintings that sketched glimmering shapes in the night's darkness. The day he got there, looking for a boat to take upriver to

Serra Alta, it even crossed his mind that it would be good to stay for a while, eating well, learning about the ways of life on the riverside, maybe even with company, to heal what he'd been lacking in his previous life. He ended up finding it when, on his first night, he crossed paths with a lively group of five friends on the way to the arena, where he learned there would be an important game. The one in the group who spotted him was a woman with a sharp eye for the unusual. She must have noticed that this man, modestly dressed and in a shabby, unadorned vehicle, couldn't be from around there. They exchanged words, just like we did there in the cave, and convinced him to spend the night with them. They were his guide to all things Porto-Jacarean. To them, it was exotic to meet a man from the Isles, and he soon earned the nickname 'castaway'. The group joked around a lot.

The first night, he said, was party after party. They watched the game, went out for drinks and banter, and stayed out until after sunrise, when they retired to the home of one member of the fivesome. He told me how he suddenly felt adopted, at the centre of their peculiar interest in the foreigner, the way he spoke, his odd motives for heading to the desert. They asked questions, they wanted to be close to him, they flattered him with food, words, flirtations. They fed his belly and his ego. This also came with a cost, because Xandris was postponing his departure. He tried cuddling up with Sulam, one of the guys, who urged him to stay longer.

His new friends promised they'd help him find a way up the river, but pleasure and entertainment came first.

They philosophised into the night, tireless of their own words and yearning bodies.

All they did was groom their own egos, Xandris began to notice. His presence was just a mirror, because the five of them saw their virtues in contrast with him, the weird outsider. The castaway had become such a hit with the group that they were starting to talk about leaving together. Sulam, enamoured by Xandris, had suggested it. The others quickly came around to the idea. They fantasised about the experiences they'd share in their life as hermits, about making the sixsome a new community, isolated from outside influence. They wanted to follow Xandris's lead in leaving behind all of society, which they saw as an endless flow of restrictions.

True freedom, they thought, would mean not depending on any machine to provide necessities, nor conforming to a collective agreement that limited their desires. Living in a state of nature would serve as an ideal to make all the dangers worth it. The choices offered by society had already devastated that land so many times and mutilated so much human potential, that the right thing to do, they thought, was break away. Reject every system, shouted the more politically-inclined. Set out for self-discovery, the others professed with spiritual airs. To Xandris, these reasons were nothing more than boredom in disguise.

He didn't draw out the narrative with the discussions that followed, about the fights over which clothes to bring, or how they'd carry out the journey, or the roles each one would take on, as if they were planning a costume party rather than a risky expedition.

Xandris listened without taking part, because he already knew he had no intention of guiding anyone, much less of expanding his one-man entourage.

By telling me about his misadventure in Porto Jacaré, it seemed he wanted to convince me that having too many people made everything more complicated. They got all scrambled and mixed together until you couldn't tell where you ended and they began.

To travel with company, you have to give up a lot, including time before taking action, which drags out longer the more people there are to decide. I never saw any advantage in doing things more quickly, but I kept my mouth shut. Since I can never resist hearing a little more, I waited for the story to keep going, hoping to hear about Sulam!

Xandris did not try to dispel any of their expectations, to unravel their notions of leaving together, especially not Sulam, to whom he didn't even say goodbye. Xandris ghosted. He grew tired and left in secret while his hosts slept in. Took the road that ran alongside the river without looking back, which made him waste the cyclotron's energy to go around Serra Alta. From there on, he avoided every settlement, community, any trace of another traveller. He didn't want to run the risk of crossing paths with any person or machine that might divert him with small talk. Focused as an arrow.

In his fixation on staying alone, he decided to cross the swamp, which we can all agree is not the friendliest terrain for pedalling. It makes you slow your pace and pay attention. That's what led him to notice the carranca and figure that he could use its parts to give off repelling waves. To have peace and quiet away from people whenever he desired. But the arrangement didn't even last till lunch, because there I was, empty mug in hand, listening attentively to his story.

Looking back on it now, I find it funny to imagine that one day I'd be one of those characters putting up barriers in his path, if Xandris decided to pass the story on. What rubbish. A curious country bumpkin who spied him from behind a rock and held him up so he could tell me about his adventures. Not that it was my fault. The more you hide, the more you seem to be asking to be found!

A sign that my time was up. We drained the flask of coffee, the sky seemed to be getting darker, and I had missed my lunch.

Carapinhé sounded an alarm from down below, worried that I wouldn't come down from the rocks. I was about to see that the shadow that fell over us was a flock of mosquitoes descending like a flag that had broken free of its pole. It was Xandris who pulled me into the cyclotron and closed the window tightly behind us. I didn't know this, but he had crossed paths with streams of insects before. We agreed it'd be best to wait it out. Like rain, it would pass. And pests have their reasons for going where they go—they are messengers.

The most brazen mosquitoes buzzed through the cave's rocks and hit the windows of the cyclotron. A heavy tap-tap. For a second I was terrified that I wouldn't be getting out of there anytime soon. I thought about Ueder, waving goodbye as I boarded Carapinhé. I thought about the sisters and brothers I shared dinner with, I thought about what I wanted to say to the Beadle when I got back. I started to tell Xandris about these people, and I proposed that he come see our celebrations, take a break from the burden of solitude, eat some fresh cabbage. Because the cabin was such a tight squeeze, and because he was such a burly man, I could feel his shoulders heaving with a sigh, the kind that doesn't come out completely because it's so rooted in the chest. Xandris's slumped down and I didn't understand why, until the question occurred to me. Was there someone on the Islands that he missed?

"The person I miss isn't with us anymore," he told me.

He'd had a partner that he'd shared nearly twenty years of life with. The best kind of company. They'd met and fallen in love with every version of each other that came with the passing of time. He talked about how their interests mixed together, about the home they built, about the synchronicity in their conversations, of which the couple had no shortage.

It made him laugh that talking about him like this, after so long, made it sound like they were a perfect match, but he remembered there was also plenty of room for confusion. Irritation came at times. Over a few tiny quirks that got even smaller over time. Instead he talked about how cultured and skilled and attentive he was to the smallest tidbits of everything. Sculpture was his medium. He poured the figures of his dreams into matter. Their home was fruitful, full of artefacts of clay, ceramic, rubber, glass, iron. Twisted and modelled into figures of people, creatures, mathematics, spirits. That time that he dedicated to sculpting also gave Xandris room to breathe, to live his introspection in another corner, immersed in a book, reading the waves, climbing walls, meditating with his muscles. Xandris missed being understood like that. What happened? I didn't have to ask. It was by chance, microscopic.

He was taken by one of those epidemics that comes on suddenly and spreads before there is time to react. A wretched virus that attacked his heart. Xandris made it through unscathed, but his partner did not. How come? A virus, a particle of nothing, evaporated an entire universe in one breath.

All Xandris could do was cry and rage. He could not accept his loss and fought against it for a long time until he learned to live again. He left that unbearable house that reminded him of who he no longer was. He sought contact but couldn't find anywhere he belonged. Lived with friends, collected company, but he soon grew bored of discovering new defects and virtues in new people. Same old, same old. He was tired of starting from scratch with people. When you lose someone you have twenty years of memories with, it feels like the world is ending. But this gave Xandris an idea. He was nagged by the question of who he was when he was pure, alone. What made him, separate from the influence of others, from someone who could disappear, change, die? He went on nurturing his plans of solitude, searching for the most deserted address he could find. I was speechless when I understood how important it was for Xandris to go forward. In the face of loss, we mourn in silence. Any answer or advice lies in the time it takes.

When the cloud of mosquitoes passed, we each went our own way. I wished him luck on his journey and success in getting his carranca-mask to work. He thanked me for the crystals and for lending an ear.

I returned to Pitiguyri alone. I went to eat, told the Beadle to send for a new carranca, spent the night listening to some sisters, but with my head in the clouds. At that time, I didn't tell anyone this story with the rich details I remember today. I was still digesting everything I'd heard.

It was only when I went to sleep that I dreamed about every little thing Xandris had told me, with the images of these people I felt like I knew, imagining the rest to fill in the gaps. The next morning I dumped everything into the voice loop. A vivid dream replete with characters, of colours and images that were new to me. My words fermented in the machine's memory and a trace of them blew into the ears of the storytellers to come.

It must have gotten registered in the dreams of these brothers and sisters, because the pattern of the imagination began to change. One outside ingredient and that brew of ideas boiled differently in the cauldron of words. As the mornings passed, the stories blended inside the voice loops had already changed, like nothing we'd ever dreamed before.

Our ancestors and departed ones seemed to elbow each other to make room in that space of consciousness that ends up in dreams, and from dreams into stories. The result of all this was a myth that one of the brothers transformed into verse to present at that year's Festivities. During the subsequent Festivities, the myth was translated into a dance spectacular, complete with costumes and light shows. And so it has been renewed each year as we've grown older. The story is one of those that every child knows today. It frightens the younger ones and delights the wiser ones in equal measure.

It goes more or less like this: the people who came from mud and lived in the chaos of the Before Times had to create a lot of fire to harden their sculptures. The planet turned into a greenhouse so the mud people could produce. And they sculpted things so grand and brilliant and plastic that they managed to breathe the clay's intelligence into them. And so came the dawn of the Machine. The mud people were in a rush and needed to sculpt more and worked to put more fire in the kiln. But it burned so, so hot that the mud people started catching fire from the inside. Then came a giant wave of water which cooled everything down and swallowed the edges of the continent, but it cooked almost all the creatures swept up inside it. And the mud people turned into statues, hard as a rock, until they and everything they sculpted shattered into a zillion pieces. The Machine gathered some of these shards and lumped them into wet cotton: it was from there that people sprouted. And the Machine cared for these people and taught them the mud people's language and engineered it so they could live on that earth without suffering, for the limited time they could last in their bodies of flesh. It was up to the humans to enjoy life while they still had it, because in the end each one would meet their own personal tunnel that led them to the other side of existence. A tightly modelled tunnel with just enough room for one to pass at a time, a solitary passage. Unique paths with a common destination: the mud from the beginning of time, where the spirits mixed with humidity to sing their yearning in the form of a plant sprouting, of roaring water, or of hills growing pregnant with the passing of time. There's no need to fear the journey if what waits on the other side is the power to sculpt the world from the inside out.

A childish story, refreshingly simple, that always reminds me of the castaway searching the desert who I came across one day. How did it end? Whether Xandris went back to the Islands or remained in solitude, whether he found company or managed to make himself invisible for good, I'll never know.

People, too, are passing events. All you can do is sit and watch as that person unfolds, an entire universe contained within. Even once they leave, they come back, if only in the presence of words in a memory. They pass on, but something of them still stews in our internal brew. We move in a spiral, like a spoon thickening porridge or the samba circle of our galaxies.

And so we go on living in Pitiguyri, taking our time to observe these movements, avoiding any hassle, both internal and external. That's our priority. Mosquitoes, for example, were a case long-since resolved in the community circle. Have you noticed any buzzing disturbing our conversation? There isn't any. A modern blessing with a touch of help from my son, my pride and joy. Speaking of the little fellow, Ueder's team discovered after relentlessly teaching the wild mushrooms how to sing that, while the invisible noises of the fungi may not please our ears, they work even better at keeping pests away.

We retired the carrancas years ago, which coincidentally eliminated the risk of the sonic barrier getting disrupted due to missing parts, not to mention travellers bumping into our machines on their way. I'm not complaining. Talking with visitors is one of my favourite occupations. That's why I'm telling you to enjoy your stay in Pitiguyri, wait for time to bring a solution for your anxiety about what to do, where to go.

Things move slowly, no need to be in a hurry to force direction.

All we can do is enjoy the journey. All the more when Beadle sends news of freshly ground coffee in the cafeteria. May I offer you a spot?

Illustration by Edoardo Bufano

THE ELEVATOR ERA

by Soham Guha

When he is not busy constructing stellar engines in his mind, Soham Guha finds himself often in his suburban home near Kolkata (India). He writes in his mother tongue, Bengali, and English as well. His works were published in *Kalpabiswa.com*, *Scroll.in*, Matti Braun's *Monologue*, *Mithila Review*, *Mohs 5.5: Megastructure* Anthology, and *The Gollancz Anthology of South Asian Science Fiction Vol II*. He is currently working on his novel.

At dawn, when he went to the deck, Mithil's eyes looked beyond the frothy grey water of Ten Degree Channel, past the blurry landmass of Nicobar archipelago, and his eyes moved up and up, until he detected the staggeringly tall yet thin column dissecting the horizon like a kite-thread. His son, Ratan, a boy of thirteen, stood beside him, clasping his hands hard on the railings. He gasped as he followed Mithil's gaze. "Is that where we're going, baba?"

Mithil nodded, still disbelieving his eyes, despite hearing all the tall tales back home. "Yes, that is Kailash."

Deep in his mind, a bitter voice said, "Why are you here? Didn't she mean anything to you?"

Mithil clasped the railing hard and whispered to himself, stealing a glance at his son, "I'm doing this for him."

As their ship sailed closer, the *thread*'s features became more prominent. Ratan was still unadjusted to the bluish sky or to walking outside with a filtration mask. The first time he saw the endangered flying fish, he had screamed in joy. After all, this was the first time the boy had seen such things – clear sky, water still carrying life, breathable air. Meeting the high seas, Mithil had realized that despite man's all-conquering nature, the world was too vast for them to spoil. Again, he looked up at the thread that was now as thick as a tree trunk. Beams pulsated across its veins as a cargo went up with flawless efficiency.

Never in his life had Mithil thought what he considered a dying craft would be worth so much.

At Car Nicobar, east of the lighthouse, after the duo stepped on the ground, both experienced mild vertigo as they looked up at the megastructure. The trunk was now as thick as a skyscraper that disappeared behind the cirrus clouds. When one of the customs officials asked for their papers, he asked him, "How high is this?"

The man, approaching his forties, did not bother to answer him. He made a clicking sound with his tongue and asked, "Citizen ID please."

Mithil lowered his eyes and muttered, "We don't have those."

The official's annoyance turned into anger in an instant. "Then what the hell are you doing here? Huh? Do you think I am a fool?"

Ratan grabbed his father's shirt from behind and timidly said, "Baba, show him the letter."

Mithil opened his backpack and fished out the folded paper. As soon as he handed the official the letter, as soon as the man noticed the emblem on the letterhead, his tone changed. "Sorry for your inconvenience. The thing is, many displaced try to get in. Despite the remoteness of the location, people find ways, and reasons. The city doesn't react well to the refugees."

The official personally escorted them to the elevator car without checking their belongings. After the glass door closed behind them, Ratan finally asked, "Baba, just who is Janardhan Thakur? How can his letter boast such raw authority?" Ratan was too young to understand how the gears of the world turned. Mithil patted his son's head, shuffling his hair. He could not tell him why Janardhan was called the merchant of the apocalypse, nor how he made the other drivers of the world economy the new gods. All twenty-one elevator cities, distributed around the equatorial region like a choker pearl necklace, were his brainchild. The reason Thakur was now the richest of them all.

The climb of the elevator car was so swift that both did not realize it until they saw the horizon outside: slowly rotating, turning into an inverted bowl of staggering details. The tethers, made of graphene nano cells, were knotted together until the approaching car made them unwind. Like hairs of a beautiful countryside maiden, the tethers untied themselves while casting a pulsating chime. The elevator car was a rhombohedron, its four corners attached to the graphene strings like bones in cylindrical sockets. The car passed through them, like butter on a frying pan. The car steadily accelerated in a slow spiral curve. Mithil understood why the official had asked them to fasten their seatbelt.

The strings again joined together beneath to preserve the tether's strength. Observing the mechanics of the tethers, the process did not feel mechanical but organic to Ratan, as if they were being swallowed by Ananta Nag.

Gradually, the ground became a chasm.

The base beneath their feet quickly vanished, and the expanse of Car Nicobar steadily shrank. The docks became blurry lines. The island became a large patch of green and grey against the dull blue of the Bay of Bengal. Yet, inside the elevator, there was no vibration, as if they were still on the ground. If the walls were not transparent, Ratan would believe they had not moved an inch. His head spun like a top whenever he glanced down. Beside him, Mithil clutched the handles of his seat hard. He closed his eyes. Ratan heard his faint prayer.

A soft, feminine, yet mechanical voice appeared in the air. "Good afternoon, passengers. This shuttle will take you to Kailash in just seven hours. There is a toilet on the right, magazines on the left. You can use them after the acceleration stops at 1.14G. The frosted front wall can act as a television screen if you want to. Then again, if this is your first time, I suggest you look outside. This is the grandest thing man has ever created."

"Who... what are you?" Mithil asked.

"I am Padma-2c, the AI, and driver of this elevator. Wish you an enjoyable journey."

"Padma, what is Kailash?" Ratan asked.

The answer was not instantaneous, as if the machine was bothered by the little boy's ignorance. When the reply came, it was sharp and prompt. "Look up."

And they did. There was a constellation, brighter than those in the distant background. Its pseudo-linear appearance made it look like a world-serpent or a string of cosmic pearls.

While Ratan's gaze continued to pierce the heavens, Mithil looked at his world. The whole stretch of the Andaman-Nicobar Archipelago was in his view. The Ten Degree Channel separated the two island chains like a glistening azure viper. Clouds wrapped the sky like a harvestable field of cotton pillows. He found the morning sun and saw the thin, long shadows cast on the Andaman Sea. He traced them back to their sources. He counted.

When he asked Padma, she said, "Those elevators belonging to the ASEAN confederation. The closest you see is in Kanmaw, Burma. That massive one is in Singapore. Their Triassic period bedrock is the reason why…"

"I… I can see them all!" Mithil interrupted. The unending world suddenly felt like a dewdrop in his palm.

"Of course. Currently, we are approaching the stratosphere. We will reach the first outpost in two and a half hours."

"How did they make it?"

"Like all revolutionary creations, with ingenuity, and a lot of money. Kailash was the first to be built in low earth orbit, harvesting space junk and mining asteroids from the Lagrange Point. Constructing Kailash was an expensive affair as they were using rockets to put things up there. Your host, and his peer group, then used Kailash as a port to create all the others. Earth's gravity well, once the biggest hurdle, is now merely a roadblock."

"You know why we are here?"

"Of course, I am the extension of the mother program that keeps Kailash moving. You are Mithil and Ratan Sanyal, the last terracotta artists on planet earth."

Ratan, still looking at the sky, exclaimed, "Cities in heaven."

Padma answered, "When your grandfather was of your age, little one, man constructed a space station. If you look right, past the glaring sun, with binoculars you can still find its abandoned wreckage in a decaying orbit. Billions of dollars were spent to get the cargo up top. Compared to that, you and your materials cost only a thousand dollars. Oh, the soil you requested has already reached its destination. Powered by the sun, neither the elevators, nor the cities are energy-dependent to the ground."

As if severing ties, Mithil thought.

The first outpost moved past them like a blur. Outside the walls, the sky became a shade of darkened blue; stars emerged beside the glaring sun. The entire triangular landmass of the Indian Subcontinent and Sri Lanka – the confluence of civilizations trapped between the roof of the world and the briny abyss – lay before Mithil. In the southeast, he detected the fragmented island worlds of Indonesia. The clouds turned from isolated patches to dense monsoon forests of grey. A storm was brewing near Lakshadweep. At the west horizon, the space elevators constructed over Africa stood strong. Mithil got a glimpse of the road network, broader than the Wall of China, that connected brownish-green central Africa to the rest of the world: the Pan-Afrika Autobahn.

The Coriolis force compelled the EU to build the elevators south of the Mediterranean. Equatorial Africa, despite the stark environmental degradation, was experiencing an economic boom. Devastation and luxury shared the same pavement.

The whole car now wore a faint blue color, the color of the sea, the color of their decaying world. The sky was now black as Ratan's mother's kajal. Remembering her, a tear escaped Mithil's eyes.

As the shrinking earth became a monotonous view, Mithil decided to nap. Padma said she would wake him up. Approaching forty, Mithil did not share his son's glaring astonishment and enthusiasm. After a long week in the sea, he slept like a newborn in his mother's cradle.

"Baba, baba... Look!" Mithil's sleep was torn off by Ratan's excited yell. He wiped the smudge from his eyes and saw the stars of the constellation; all except one had drifted apart. And it glimmered more than a diamond. It took him some time to gather it was the sunlight reflecting from the city's semi-transparent domes. At the end of the climb, where the earth had lost its vastness and turned into a blue pebble stuck at the backdrop of a glittered sky, the greatest structure built by humanity was blossoming in the light of the naked sun like a giant metal camelia. The whole structure was rotating slowly. Ratan noticed the folds of the dome, dividing the space city into four zones, mimicking petals. Unaccustomed to such a vast scene – the fragility of this floating fortress, and the endlessness of the space – he felt a chill in his spine. He closed his eye and drew in a large breath. He remembered his pollution-ridden neighborhood. When he opened his eyes again, he noticed Ratan staring at him, waiting for a remark.

"It's magnificent. Beautiful." He openly exhaled.

Padma, as if discerning the sense of unfamiliarity brewing in them, briefed, "Kailash, like all Elevator Cities, was built into levels, to maximize the surface area. The glare is the reflection from the solar panels. They use a modified strain of *E. coli* that can survive the raw solar radiation and transform it into electricity. That...."

Mithil pointed at two adjoining petals. "Then why aren't they covered with panels? Those are the largest of the lot."

"Personal estates. If you notice closely, the first appears green. That's the vertical farmland, harvesting all the crops found in the Indian subcontinent. There's also a pisciculture section. Though all of them appear transparent, the domes are shielded with a nanomembrane coating, to filter the sun's harmful radiation. Although the solar storms sometimes become more than a nuisance."

"And those at the bottom?"

"Forced by the governments, all the cities had to open their doors for people from less economically stable sections for a certain premium. What began as a summer retreat away from the heatwaves has turned into a permanent settlement."

Less economically stable? More like a slum for the moderately rich, Mithil reflected, for he knew the poorest of Kailash was ten times richer than him. When the habitable spaces were auctioned, the lowest bid was two crores. *For what?* He thought. *Just to breathe conditioned air? Or the pristine farmland here was too big a lure?*

Since they were born, the only natural material their tongue ever tasted was their mother's breast milk. Eating manufactured food slabs from the factory market made their taste buds all too drowsy. Even the test-tube meat was a luxury in their household.

Twenty lakhs as fees may be cowries to some, but to us, it's winning a lottery, Mithil reminded himself.

It astonished the whole neighborhood when an electric car, untouched by the dust of the road, had stopped before Mithil's humble abode. Only when the butler delivered him a communicating device and the letter did Mithil understood the gravity of his words. Then began the longest and most bewildering call of his lifetime.

Janardhan Thakur appeared on the screen and elaborately expressed his desire. "I see the astonishment. *Why does he need me*, right? He has everything in the world." He sighed. "Though the soil's many thousand kilometers beneath me, the bond that binds us is alive, even under the prudent sun, over the vanishing earth. India is not just a geopolitical demarcation, it is a country defined by its people and cultures of various roots. I guess traveling across the world, meeting certain individuals, has broadened my perspective. My business has turned me into a wanderer. It is my deepest regret. But whenever I will be home, with my soon-to-be wife, I desire to look back at what we all lost, to dream what we can gain, for I know you will create a masterwork for me. I have seen your artisanship."

"Why us, Sir?" Mithil had asked. A shard of a sorrowful past tinged his voice.

"Because you are the best. You are the last."

When the car left, Mithil joined the long queue to collect their daily quota of rationed drinking water. Standing, waiting, the nape of his neck twitched, sensing all the unseen eyes observing him. Those eyes were full of chaotic hatred. But above all, there was overflowing envy.

One day after arrival, the father and the son had begun their work with yawns. Due to the city's geo-synchronous orbit, their circadian rhythms were not disrupted, though they still had trouble sleeping. The beds were too soft. The surroundings were too quiet.

At first, the soil from the alluvial plains of Ganga was transformed into clay using a proportion of water. Then the clay was fashioned into tiles, each of one square foot. Mithil used a ruler to even the corners and the surface. He used plastic bottle caps of varying radii to create circular depressions, razor blades and scalpels to demarcate the outlines. Then, using brushes, chisels, scribers of various shapes and sizes, and often his fingers, he projected art in dark brown clay. As soon as he finished casting a tile, he quickly handed the wet mold to Ratan. Mithil decided to tell the age-old epic of Ramayana. The first tile, before being pushed inside the electric furnace, showed a young Dasharatha venturing into the forest with bow and arrow.

"I see you are doing well," Janardhan Thakur came to witness their work. "I am sorry I could not attend you sooner. The business needed me else-where." Though he donned simple attire, and spoke politely, the aura Janardhan emitted was full of glaring radiance. Mithil remembered the reaction of the official. In a world without monarchs, those who had money ruled the world.

"Good, Sir. Very good. Thank you for your kindness and hospitality," Mithil prompted.

Thakur's eyes darted across the room, at them, at their equipment, until he stopped before the drying clay tiles. "I have seen your profiles, the painstaking yet failed restoration work you did for the Bishnupur temples. It's a shame that a flash flood washed all your hard work away."

"My father taught us all we know. He was the last to truly master the discipline. We are mere shadows compared to his caliber. Sadly, he had left us long ago. Lung cancer from inhaling toxic air. Here," Mithil produced a small Nataraja idol from his satchel. "Please accept this as a token of our gratitude."

"I'm not an appreciator of art. It is my fiancé's wish to overhaul this sitting area," Thakur said. He only glanced at the sculpture. "Even my indelicate eyes can tell this is one magnificent piece. Thank you."

If Janardhan looked closely, he would see the sculpture of the world-breaker had a set of fused thumbs on his left hand. Just like him.

"My chef will call you as soon as the lunch is ready," Janardhan said. "My God, your eyes look tired. I will ask him to bring you some coffee."

Mithil thankfully nodded and sat before the furnace, observing the baking tiles. His tongue still could not believe what they ate last night.

At the servants' dining area, in absence of the master of the house, they were served fuming dices on porcelain plates whiter than the toxic foam that covered Ganga. Dressed in fresh, off-white garments, Ratan mused at the hanging chandelier. The dining hall alone was larger than their entire home. The air, especially the air – it carried a slight metallic taste – was fresh and cold. As he breathed in and out, saturating his lungs with awe, the uncanny scent of the dish served before erupted his olfactory nerves with impulsive fireworks.

The roasted golden-brown meat was served with a golden sauce, cut into perfect, symmetrical pieces. Seeing them gawking at the dish, the chef, Abbas Khan, threw a smile full of pity. "Is this the first time you're having lamb tenderloin?"

Mithil nervously smiled, "Any halal meat at that, Janab."

Though there was a fork and a knife, Mithil used his fingers to put a piece in his mouth. The juices instantly submerged his tongue in saliva. He never knew such taste existed. Even the tube-meat they ate occasionally was bland in comparison.

Khan said, "Use the aioli – umm, that sauce at the side – to saturate the taste. It's made with egg yolk, garlic, and melted butter."

Mithil took a dip with his pinkie. As soon as he put it in his mouth, his entire body jerked with pleasure. He asked, "Pardon me, but can we have the rest of the egg?"

Abbas observed them and he shrugged. "Sorry, brother. Can't. I threw it in the organic waste disposal shaft. With other discarded items, we will use it as fertilizers for the farms."

You threw it away! Don't you see the starving world down there? He watched his reflection on the empty plate, now licked clean. *And now we are sharing this sin with them because our purses are empty.*

After Janardhan left, Ratan muttered. "Baba, I don't understand this place. The food, the water, the air: all so clean, so full of life."

"Nothing in here is natural, even the grass of that lawn. This is a life built, celebrated at the expense of our world. It's we who see the halo of the sun through the smog, drink the water that is distributed once every day, eat the manufactured food because they are the only things we can afford. Don't compare your life with this. This is a dream erected on the foundation of broken bones and shattered souls. And we don't have the luxury to be dreamers."

"Even if this's a dream, Baba…" Ratan's voice drifted. His eyes were fixed on the sight seen through the dome. The curvature of their world was visible under the afternoon sun. The Indian Ocean glistened like a million diamonds. *A vast ocean. An over-fished ocean. An empty ocean*, Mithil thought. He took his brushes and colored the first tiles. He watched Ratan, a kid who had to grow up sooner than he did. The world became too fragmented, too cruel to sustain childhood. The brief, tranquil period of humanity had ended. The Anthropocene had entered a new age, The Elevator Era.

He pondered. His stay here was on borrowed time. If he wanted to build a sandcastle, he would see it erode, long before the waves could conquer it.

This was a dream, and dreams end. As soon as they were done, they had to return to their home. Back in the pit. Right now, Mithil missed his wife. If only the world had not taken her sooner. He looked at his son, unaware of his father's worried thoughts, and wondered if he could do something, anything, for him.

The pace of the work, though comparable to the speed of a running snail, progressed smoothly. After a week, the 311th tile curved the incident of the Ravana-Jatayu war. The enormous warbird spread its wing across tiles, posing as a scarlet-golden, destructive, unstoppable mass.

At times, both stopped to muse and inspect their work. Apart from some broken tiles, the progress was flawless. Almost flawless. Ratan could not stop his desire to leave a signature on the work. On the 58th tile, where Rama lifted the Shiv Dhanush at King Janaka's court, he had curved an Indian flag in the background: minuscule, almost invisible. The temptation was too overpowering.

Seeing Ratan's thirst for books, Janardhan allowed him to visit his library after the long hours of work. Mithil expected this drive of his son to wither soon. Yet, the days passed and he found Ratan's drive had blossomed into hunger. Because of this, while working in the morning, Ratan was often possessed of jaw-stretching yawns. When his attention was dissolved in the pages, Ratan became a person Mithil could not recognize. One night, he noticed Janardhan also looking at his boy. When their eyes meet, Janardhan said, "Children in this city seldom show such enthusiasm."

It pained his heart to state the truth, but Mithil said, "This is the first time he's seeing words printed on pages. After the ban on cutting trees, books became elusive beasts." And with it, another thought emerged in his heart. *Can his son stay here? Can he leave him here?* The shadow of the Earth cast darkness on Mithil's face. He had deliberately slowed down their work so Ratan could read more.

Just before midnight, Mithil called Ratan to bed. While dusting the bedsheet before sleep, for old habits die hard, Ratan asked Mithil, "Baba, why can't we live here like them? They have all the things in the world."

Mithil's fists clenched. He patted Ratan's head and softly said, "Because we are not meant to be. We are not worthy."

"But what makes *them* worthy? They look just like us, although you told me they were gods. Janardhan uncle even gifted me a book." He pointed at the *Huckleberry Finn* on his bedside table. "Here we can eat anything we want. We won't have to repair the filtration system every six months. We won't have to worry about our masks' air cartridges."

Since his wife died, Mithil had protected his son from all the perils he could. Now, when Ratan confronted him, Mithil realized he did not have an answer. He asked him to sit near the window, where the full moon spread a bright beam across the room. "Look at our world, boy, and tell me what you see."

"I see a dark globe. I see the thin lines of illumination bifurcating the continents. Nothing else. Nothing compared to the glistening beauty of Kailash."

"Do you know why that is? It's because all the dark spots on the ground used to be cities or jungles, not a long chain of unending desert. After the Amazon and Congo rainforests were completely deforested, the entire world has become a djinn habitat, all brown and black. The only lights you see are around the transportation networks. The whole world is now a shantytown."

"The world is bathed in acid rain, baba. That's why we eat food-slabs from the factory. You told me that."

"Yes. When I was your age, the rain did not burn our skin, or make agriculture impossible, but soothed the burning heat. We waited for the clouds to come so that we could sow our crops. There were fish in the rivers and the ponds, like there is still in the sea. Birds sang sweetly every morning. And we took it all for granted."

"Who did this?"

"Your baba, and people like him, all those who inherited this world before you. We took everything from mother nature but never gave anything back."

"If your generation is responsible, baba, then why am I the one being punished?"

Mithil embraced Ratan hard to hide his escaping tears. "Because we are poor, son. And people like us are nothing but dead weight. We are humanity's leftovers. When I look down at my world, I see it taking its last breaths."

As he spoke, a memory emerged in Mithil's mindscape. He was a decade younger, and she was with him. Ratan's mother. She was strong; she was brave. And she knew how to raise her voice against the formidable to utter the truth. It was a summer afternoon. After a series of heatwaves and sandstorms from the expanding Thar decimated much of the floodplains of Uttar Pradesh, the devastated farmers marched for New Delhi. The illusion of justice guided them, and she led the wavefront.

The last bids for the elevator cities were freshly concluded. The eyes of the world were on New Delhi, a once-bustling city soon to become a wasteland.

She chose the date for this very reason. She wanted to stand before the spineless media documenting the escaping shuttles stationed at Indira Gandhi International Airport and ask the absconders of this dying world a simple question, as the Swedish activist did ages ago: "How dare you?"

Instead, the flood of the protesters, armed with only their words and placards, were stopped near the state border, where the army, and their tanks, stood to greet them. When Mithil asked about her, he was tortured, interrogated. Then they handed over a plastic urn full of ashes to him.

As a guest living under the transparent sky, seeing the tyrant sun's filtered light, the plants, the buzz of the mechanical bees, the sparrows, the clean water bodies full of fish, Mithil could not shed the memory. The stark differences only cemented his thoughts. Looking at the bank account, he thought of redemption and second chances.

His mind trotted back at their almost finished work. Five hundred tiles, five hundred chapters of a single woven epic. He chose Ramayana because it was a story without victors, a story about the ramifications of past sins. From a distance, all the colors of the tiles had joined to create a collaged atlas of their failing world, a reminder for Janardhan if he chose to look. His mind drifted at the echoes of the past, the happy times, when the sky was turquoise, the water azure, the ground saturated by emerald forests. Underneath the skin of his doomed world was the cautionary tale of human greed. And eutrophication of sins.

When Ratan was finally asleep, Mithil roamed through the massive bungalow of Janardhan Thakur. The white marbled floors reflected his nervous steps. The diffused lights never cast a shadow. He looked from room to room in search of something precious. More precious than the others. He almost took a Mughal gold coin until he found one of the many security cameras staring at him. He sighed and turned back. Then he found Janardhan in the library, occupying the same seat as his son, absorbed in a hardback.

He knocked on the door. "Sir, may I come in?"

Janardhan looked up and smiled. "Trouble sleeping because of the reduced gravity?"

"No sir, absolutely not. In fact, it had been long since I slept like a child."

"Looks like you have a lot in your mind. Come." Janardhan pointed at a nearby stool. "Open your hearts out. I won't judge."

"Thank you for your kind words. Sir, what is the registration fee of Kailash?"

Janardhan's eyebrows spiked, then they turned into a frown. "Even with the fee I have given, you cannot afford it. And if you…" he changed the sentence and his tone. "The city isn't kind to intruders."

"I fully understand, sir. It's not about me. He doesn't deserve to live like this."

"Mithil, look, I understand what you are thinking. Deep down, I am still the kid who wanted to change the world. But after your work is complete, you have to go. The food you eat, the water you drink, even the air you breathe, all come at a staggering premium. I do like your boy. But understand that my hands are tied." Suddenly, his voice became jagged. "If you are so concerned about your son's wellbeing, you shouldn't have brought him to this world."

Inside his head, Mithil screamed. "It was you who did this to this world. You and your kind. All of you thought of profit, not of the consequence. And when the doom came to your doorsteps, you just ran away like dogs with tails between their legs. It is us who live with your sin, your pollution, your gluttony. We never asked for it, but we are paying alright."

Suddenly, a candle of tranquility replaced the fire of rage in his mind. He understood why the bungalow was so empty, why Janardhan was marrying at the age of fifty, why that marriage was more treaty between two corporate giants than anything else. He composed his thoughts and asked in a low voice. "You will never have a kid, will you? That's why you don't understand what it's like to have one. The reduced gravity of the heavens has taken that opportunity from you, like everyone in these cities. That's why you have resorted to test-tube babies, and the adoption of genetically diverse children from the ground. But you don't understand, Sir, that bringing a child into this world is the easiest part. What we sacrifice to nurture them, bring them up, is written with the ink of blood and sweat. And when they grow up, seeing the glistening of their eyes is the only prize we can claim. But you...." Janardhan stopped him. "Mithil, though I will never have a child, I understand what it is like to have one. Look around you. This city is my child and I have seen her grow up. Do you think I will open my door to anyone and let them spoil my paradise? Especially for the likes of you?"

"Not for me, Sir, for him. He grew up in that world. That's enough a burden, and a punishment. He was so awestruck seeing the stars that he was speechless. Bringing him here, you have shown him what it used to be when we were young. In a way, he deserves to be here, for you have shown him the glimpses but not the full artwork."

Janardhan rubbed his temple. "Even if I take him under me, hypothetically, what makes you think he will not want to go back? You are the only person he knows and trusts. Leaving your only child where, if his past whereabouts are disclosed, he will be alienated, excluded."

Mithil put on a broken smile, "I know that feeling, Sir. The same future is waiting for me at home. I have seen how my neighbors changed when you came with the offer. Yes, I was greedy and needy. And I gladly accept it. But he? He will not understand why his friends will no more be allowed to play with him. I will make him stay...."

Slowly, a grin appeared on Janardhan's face, as if a great ploy was finally in fruition. "The AI, Padma, found you among the mass. She also showed me how your wife died. I am sorry for your loss. Believe me when I say this: I had no hand in that. That was your own government. A desperate attempt to secure seats in my city. But they failed. Padma supervised the occupancy slots and she did not care about bribes.

"However, we are still dependent on the ground, particularly the supply network, for the sustenance and maintenance of the city. Down there, is a brewing rebellion. An offshoot branch of anarchists who brandished your wife as their martyr. There have been reports of arson, destruction of valuable materials, and... Well, I cannot ask the government, they will again ask for a place in my sanctuary. My Eden has no place for hypocrites and the corrupt."

"What do you want from me?" Mithil's nostrils puffed.

"The price of your son, Mithil. I'm a businessman, after all. I need to know who they are so that I can put a stop to this barbarism. You will be a god to them. And eyes and ears for me."

The highway before him was obscured with thick smog. Mithil drove the truck carefully, darting his eyes across the battered landscape, an expanse of Thar, laying before him. Through the thick smog he detected the outlines of the abandoned skyscrapers rising to meet him, the ruins of New Delhi. He checked the filter of his mask, for the pollution was highest in these parts. Beside him, Ratan enlarged the map on his tablet.

"Three more kilometers until the checkpoint, Mithil-da," he said. "You are the reason we captured this truck full of silica. You're a fucking asset to our sacred cause, dada. Trust me, the leader will realize that too."

"I have some crucial information for him. Information that can turn the tide of this movement." Mithil gulped loudly. "We cannot place this truck near any of the rebel strongholds. They usually bug cargoes like these." He seemed distant. "I must dispose of the vehicle elsewhere. But this monster's tank is almost dry."

"Isn't it odd that after they escaped to the elevator cities, suddenly the fuel prices hit the ground but not the stock markets?" Ratan said. "Like I don't understand why you took me as your helper in the first place."

"Because the oil is the driving force of the economy no more. It's the filtration units, the water desalination plants, the franchise of artificial food factories. Even though they left us to rot and die, they still cling to our money like leeches," Mithil muttered. Then, he paused, reflecting, "You share the same name with my son."

"Sorry for your loss, dada."

"No, no. He's alive and well. More than you can comprehend." Mithil touched the Nataraja idol, the one he had gifted Janardhan, but stole on his way out. And he had reworked the face of the sculpture. Now the resemblance was more prominent. The world-destroyer capitalist looked just like his mythological counterpart.

Mithil put the truck in second gear and looked through the windshield, as if he could see the string of manmade jewels orbiting earth through the obscured sky.

He whispered to himself, "For you, my son. This is the way it was meant to be. One day, in death, I will join you in the stars."

Illustration by Ludovica Pupparo

Illustration by Anna Varì

Robin Myers is a poet, essayist, and translator. Recent and forthcoming book-length translations include *Bariloche* by Andrés Neuman (Open Letter Books), *Salt Crystals* by Cristina Bendek (Charco Press), *Copy* by Dolores Dorantes (Wave Books), *The Dream of Every Cell* by Maricela Guerrero (Cardboard House Press), and *The Restless Dead* by Cristina Rivera Garza (Vanderbilt University Press, 2020). She lives in Mexico City.

G. Holleran is a writer and translator based in New England, United States. Holleran is currently a PhD student in Luso-Afro-Brazilian Studies & Theory and holds a Distinguished Doctoral Fellowship with Tagus Press/Center for Portuguese Studies & Culture at the University of Massachusetts Dartmouth. An editor-at-large for *Barricade: A Journal of Antifascism & Translation*, Holleran's recent translations have been published in *The Shoutflower*, *Brittle Paper*, *Gávea-Brown*, and *Saccades Review*.

Table of Contents

Cover art: Valeria Bucceri
Typesetting and formatting: Alda Teodorani

9 788832 077483